Camellia The Bald

E.W. Zrudlo

Coastal Carolina Press
www.coastalcarolinapress.org

First edition 2001

Cover and book design by Robert Bunch, Intrepid Media
Original illustrations by Thomas Fleming

Applied for Library of Congress Cataloging-in-Publication Data

Printed In Canada

ISBN 1-928556-31-0

To the real Susan,
who began it so many years ago
with her request for a story.

And to Mallory,
who hoped.

ACKNOWLEDGEMENTS

Writing a story that becomes a book is consuming, frustrating and isolating, but fulfilling too. It requires the help of many people other than the writer, some of them unaware of their contributions, the family and friends whose simple faith—"Of course you'll finish"—is often the only ground the writer stands on. Thanks to Erika, Susan, Mom, Alan, David, Robbin and Stefanny. Most especially to Barb, best of sisters. And Richard—where do such friends come from?

Without Emily, whose last name will forever be Editor, not Colin, the story would be back in my drawer and rattling around in my head. She saw more clearly than anyone, I think, what the story might be. With timely praise, irritating questions and fearless criticism, she got me to do what I hoped I could.

The marvelous folks at Coastal not only stood behind Emily but also actively encouraged me whenever, harried and haggard, I arrived with my latest efforts.

Lastly, I thank Carolina itself, my home of hard lessons and soft air.

CHAPTER ONE

HOME

Aunt Camellia had sent the Persian carpet just last year. The delivery men pulled it from the truck, heaved it to their shoulders like a sagging log and marched into the house. Susan weaved in and out of their legs, anxious to see it unrolled.

"For goodness' sake, child, get out of the way," her mother scolded. "It's only a carpet." Mrs. Cardiff scanned the invoice and her mouth turned down. "From Aunt Camellia."

"Aunt Camellia?" Susan peered at the paper in her mother's hand, hoping to see a picture of the carpet. "I bet it's beautiful!"

Her mother sniffed, told the men to put their delivery in the living room entrance, and signed the bill.

"Aren't you going to cut the strings and unroll it?" Susan danced on and off the carpet, willing the shaggy pieces of hemp to burst of their own accord.

"Certainly not. I have no intention of re-arranging my furniture to gratify your aunt or your curiosity."

"I'll help. It'll only take a minute." Susan bounded to the French provincial coffee table and began to shove it towards the side of the room.

"Stop it!" Her mother rushed over. "You'll break my ornaments. Neither you nor your father ever cares about what I want. You just plunge in and do whatever you feel like."

Delight had drained from Susan's face. Not for the first time, she wondered where the mother who had been full of fun and laughter had gone, replaced by this other one who bossed her around like a bad teacher.

"Go out and play."

Susan waited till the screen door slammed behind her before saying anything. "Ornaments! Stupid crystal birds. Serve them right if they did break, they're so ugly."

She scuffed her way across the front yard, then headed to her apple tree and climbed into a comfortable crook. She'd discovered the tree when they'd moved in four years ago. It had been hidden by a wild growth of raspberry canes and young poplars. Helping her father cut them away, she'd found another treasure—an antique wrought-iron insignia half-buried in the ground, still attached to its rotting post. She and her father had dug it out and brought the rusty masterpiece in triumph to her mother, clods of dirt clinging to the design's loops and curls.

Mrs. Cardiff had wrinkled her face in disgust. "More trash. All I've done since we bought this hundred-year-old disaster is scrub and clean and pull off wallpaper and throw out rubbish. We're going to have to rip up the carpeting—I can't get it clean, Harold, I just can't. There are stains everywhere. The whole place is a sty. And look at the wilderness out here—vines and brambles and weeds and bushes everywhere. We'll never have a proper yard. I don't know why we moved."

"But Ann, we wanted this place. That's what we saved for. 'An adventure,' we said. Remember?"

Her mother had burst into tears. "Why can't things just be nice?" she wailed, running into the house. They heard her feet pound up the stairs.

Her father's shoulders slumped, his head hanging in despair. The buried treasure that had kindled her mother's tantrum drooped in his hand. Susan pitied her father, herself and the life they now lived because the woman they both loved didn't seem to love them anymore. She touched her father's fingers.

"Je pense qu'il est joli, Papa." I think it's pretty.

Susan always talked to her father in French. He'd spoken it to her for as long as she could remember; it was their language. Until Mrs. Cardiff's personality changed, Susan never thought much about the fact that her mother didn't know French very well. One day she asked about this.

"Why don't you talk French, Mommy?"

"Not that it's any of your business, but I'll tell you anyway. It gave me headaches, so I stopped. I have more than enough to worry about without adding French to the list."

Susan had asked Papa the same question later, when her mother wasn't around. He massaged his cheeks as he answered. "I don't really know, Sue C. She took lessons and was making good progress too. She quit about the same time she didn't want to go to my conferences with me. She said the flights gave her migraines.

4

When I said I thought she should go to the doctor just to, you know, check things out, her…ah, rather loud response made me…concerned. 'So now I'm crazy just because I can't learn your stupid French!' she said."

"I don't understand." Susan had frowned.

"I'm not sure but I think it has to do with her family's history of mental illness."

"I didn't know that."

"It's not something she or anyone for that matter would talk about much, is it? At any rate, in the past, a number of Mommy's relatives died in asylums, you see. It's a safe bet many of them were misdiagnosed and called crazy because doctors in those days simply didn't know what was wrong. But she doesn't want to be one of the crazies in her family, and she's afraid if she goes to the doctor he'll tell her she is. So we have to be brave and wait for her to find the courage to go to the doctor herself. We can't make her."

After that Susan tried to be brave, but it was hard. More and more she turned to her father for the love and fun her mother used to give.

"Let's wash the whatever-it-is, Papa, and see what

it is."

He placed the back of his free hand against her cheek. *"Ma petite étoile."* My little star.

"Maybe we could get a new post for it."

His good spirits returned as they chattered happily and cleaned their treasure.

Susan eyed the rusty winged creature their washing had revealed. "Could we paint it gold?"

"An excellent choice for a phoenix."

"Phoenix?"

Her father had told her the story of the Arabian bird. At the end of its thousand-year life it made a nest of spice tree branches. Then it set fire to its nest while it was still in it and burned itself to ashes. At dawn the next day the phoenix rose from its ashes to live another thousand years. It did this forever, living, dying and rising again.

Papa had gone to the hardware store and returned with a new post and a can of gold paint. First he drove in the post where the old one had stood; then he attached the wrought-iron phoenix, and Susan painted it gold. When they'd stood back to admire their work, though, something didn't look quite right.

"The post," Susan decided. "It's too light. The phoenix doesn't stand out. A red post would be better."

The red post made the phoenix look like it was flying out of a fire.

"It's risen again, Papa. Just like in the story."

"What!" came her mother's exasperated cry. She'd walked up behind them. "I'm turning into an old woman cleaning this wretched house and what are you two doing? Playing, that's what. Couldn't it have waited till your work was done? Look at the mess in the yard. Branches everywhere. Can't you do a single thing I ask? What's the point of telling you two anything?"

Her father put his arm around her mother's shoulder. "Ann…"

She shrugged it off as though it were a snake. "Don't touch me! Just do what you're told."

So Susan and Papa had done their work. When they finished cutting the saplings and thorny canes and made a pile, her father sprinkled gas on them and tossed in a match. Flames jumped from the pile with a *whooof*! Susan loved the sound and the sudden heat. She and her father stood together for a few minutes, staring into the blaze.

"Can you tend the fire while I go talk to your mother?"

Susan had nodded and found a stick to prod it with. As the pile burned down and the smoke grew less dense, she contemplated the wrought-iron phoenix through the smoke and shimmering heat.

"I wish I could see a real one. Maybe it would let me ride on its back, and I could live for a thousand years too." She stabbed the coals with her stick. "With no mother to hate me."

And so Susan's life went. Knowing her mother was suffering didn't help when her mother treated her cruelly; it made her angry. "Why should I pretend it's okay when it's not? *That's* crazy."

On the day the Persian carpet was delivered, her father had shared Susan's enthusiasm for it. "Of course it'll be marvelous. Would Aunt Camellia give us anything that wasn't? Look at the painting she sent a few years back."

Susan's mother grudgingly agreed about the painting and, after she'd secured her "things," they all shifted the furniture, clearing a spot for the carpet. Susan snipped the cords and unrolled it. She leapt onto the luxuriously thick carpet, prancing along the winding design to the golden flower at the center. As she stood on it, she felt a curious tingling.

"Maybe it's a flying carpet." Susan's head was full of the stories she'd devoured in *A Thousand and One Nights*, which Papa had given to her after they'd found the wrought-iron phoenix. She yanked off her shoes and socks and danced her bare feet along the path of circles. "It's so soft. You try, Papa." She held out her hand to him.

He was with her in an instant, shoes and socks off, walking the circles to Susan at the center. They'd turned to Mrs. Cardiff.

"C'mon, Mom."

"Yes, Ann, it really does feel wonderful."

Her mother's smile and words flooded Susan with happy memories. "You're a pair of the silliest geese. I don't know what I'm going to do with you."

"Join us," Papa said.

And she did, removing her shoes and neatly placing her socks inside them.

"Follow the circles," Susan insisted, pulling her mother through the maze to the center. "Isn't this the most amazing carpet?"

"It is nice," her mother admitted. "It's very red, though."

"But it's not overpowering, Ann. See how well it looks on your new wall-to-wall carpeting."

"Yes, there is that. I don't suppose there'll be much harm in trying it for a while."

"Yay!" Susan hugged her mother.

When some of her father's friends marveled at Aunt Camellia's gift, Susan heard no further talk from her mother about rolling it up or putting it somewhere else. The only problem was that Mrs. Cardiff put the furniture back on it, placing her coffee table right over the gold-flower center. When the couch and chairs were rearranged, Susan couldn't walk the path through the circles. She took to pushing the furniture off when her mother was out. Once she was caught.

"What do you think you're doing?"

"Just walking the circles."

"Put my furniture back this instant, and don't you ever do it again."

But Susan *had* done it again. She'd chosen her moments more carefully, that was all. Today, with Papa gone and her mother on her worst rampage, Susan wanted to free the carpet from her mother's furniture, fly away on it and be anywhere but in this prison, her home.

She'd been 'caught' in the boat shed sanding a plank of the sailboat she and her father were building. She seethed with the unfairness of being punished for it. Her father was in Paris giving a paper on Pythagoras, the number thirteen, and the design of gothic cathedrals. When she'd learned he would stay to do some research, she'd begged to go with him.

"Now, Sue C.," he said—he always included the initial of the name she shared with his famous Aunt Camellia, her great aunt—"you know you can't come. Next year, when you're thirteen, that's what we agreed. Besides, my stay overlaps the time you usually go to one of those camps."

"But Mommy's meaner when you're away."

"Sweetie…"

"She *is*!"

Her father grimaced and ran a hand through his hair. "I know it's hard, but try to understand that she doesn't want to be that way. Remember, something's the matter with her, Sue C., and she's afraid to go to the doctor to find out. Just hang on until I get back and we'll work on it, okay?"

Then her father opened his arms to her and, though she resisted a few seconds, she entered their comfort. They talked about their boat and where they'd sail it.

Because she missed her father and was feeling lonely, Susan had gone to the boat shed and worked on their boat—to feel close to him. And of course her mother had found her. She'd rushed in screaming that Susan wasn't allowed there without her father around. "Whatever possessed you?"

She'd only been sanding, for goodness' sakes. *"Franchement t'exagérès!"* she'd replied saucily. Stop being silly.

Mrs. Cardiff's face first turned white, then scarlet. She'd grabbed a two-foot scrap of wood and smacked

Susan on the leg. Susan stiffened in shock. Her mother had never hit her before. Mrs. Cardiff marched her into the house and ordered Susan to work in the living room the rest of the day. "First, take down every one of those precious books your hoity-toity aunt has sent and dust them. Then put them back according to their size. Only one size per shelf, do you understand? I'm sick of the mess you and your father make of the bookshelves."

"But books are supposed to look…"

"Don't argue with me! If you don't have enough books the same size to fill the shelf, go get some of your father's."

"Move Papa's books?" Susan was appalled.

Mrs. Cardiff suddenly pressed the heels of her hands into her forehead, her eyes squeezed shut. "Oh…" She bent over in anguish.

"Are you all right, Mom?" Susan rushed to her mother, peering at her bowed head, touching her arm. "Mom?"

At last her mother had raised her head, dragging her hands down a face transformed into a mask of pain. She opened her eyes and focused on Susan. "Do as you're told!" she'd exploded. "When you're finished, read that last book your aunt sent, but only when those shelves look the way they're supposed to." She'd yanked her arm away from Susan's touch and staggered upstairs, hands back on her forehead.

Susan felt whipped. For minutes she stood numbly in the living room; then she'd begun to seethe at her life's unfairness. "I hate her," she whispered.

She also feared her, and set about her work, oblivious to her mother's movements. She took down the books, dusted them and rearranged them, every shelf filled with books of identical heights. "They look fake now," she muttered hours later. "Or boring like encyclopedias or law books." Using her task as an excuse to push the coffee table off the Persian carpet, she'd sat on the golden flower, opened her book and escaped into the life of Queen Elizabeth I. The phone's insistent ringing pulled her back into reality.

"Susan!" Mrs. Cardiff screeched from the kitchen. "Answer the phone!"

Susan lowered her head, pretending to be absorbed in her book.

Her mother stormed out of the kitchen and into the dining room with quick, heavy steps. She brandished a wooden spoon laden with chocolate- chip-mottled dough. Rage flashed in her dark eyes. Stopping beside the phone table next to the stairs, she glowered at her daughter.

"Susan Camellia!"

Susan cringed. Then she felt anger burn up her timidity. How dare her mother scream at her like that! And to threaten her with the chocolate chip spoon, a symbol of their good times when they used to mix cookie batter, laugh and flick sticky chocolate chips at each other.

Straining to keep her anger in check, she rose from lotus position by simply straightening her legs. Ever since she'd mastered it in yoga class years ago, she'd been performing the feat of balance and flexibility. At first she'd done it to show off, but she came to prefer the efficiency of dropping into lotus and rising out of it, and now it was natural to her. She glared at her mother, jaw thrust forward, hands clenched in fists at her sides.

The phone rang again, the sound a momentary referee between Susan and her mother. Mrs. Cardiff narrowed her eyes. "If they hang up, you'll think the trouble

you're in now is nothing."

She dared to hope the phone *would* stop ringing just as her mother touched it. But it didn't.

"Hello?" There wasn't a hint of anger in Mrs. Cardiff's voice.

Susan bristled at her mother's self-control and politeness towards strangers. What about her own family? Didn't they deserve the same courtesy?

"Hello... Yes, this is she... Hello? Is anyone...?"

When Susan saw her mother's shoulders sag in disappointment, she felt some spiteful pleasure. What could be worse than rushing to the phone only to find someone who didn't want to talk to you? Her vengeance was short-lived, however.

"Aunt Camellia! How nice to hear from you! Who was that other woman?... Oh, I see. Your maid."

Although she'd been expecting to hear from her aunt, especially after her father had mentioned it was about that time of year, Susan wasn't sure how she felt now that the call had come. What it meant was that she'd soon be departing for somewhere, which was good because she'd get to leave her mother. But Susan had been hoping Aunt Camellia wouldn't call till after her father had returned, which would allow them some time together before she left for wherever she was going this year.

She didn't care if she *was* Aunt Camellia's favorite relative, as her father always told her. So what if Aunt Camellia was incredibly rich and paid for lessons in yoga, dance and karate, and gave her fascinating books, and sent her on month-long courses to learn white-water canoeing, rock-climbing and survival camping? All Susan knew was that she felt miserable and very sorry for herself.

"No, no, Aunt Camellia," Mrs. Cardiff lied, "you didn't catch me at a bad moment. I was…just outside in the garden, that's all. I've been expecting your call."

Susan perked up at that and strained to hear what her aunt was saying. She watched as her mother smiled and nodded.

"Yes, I think it's a *wonderful* idea. Thank you so much, Aunt Camellia. Goodbye."

She hummed a happy little tune as she hung up. "That was your Aunt Camellia," she said unnecessarily, licking the wooden spoon as she returned to the kitchen.

Susan remained standing on the Persian carpet, her book dangling from her hand.

CHAPTER TWO

GOING AWAY

When Mrs. Cardiff returned a minute later, Susan still stood in the living room, waiting to hear her fate.

"Don't stand there like a piece of wood. Get upstairs and take a shower. That was your Aunt Camellia—you've got to get packed." She clapped her hands twice, as if commanding a servant. "Get moving. Your flight leaves in three hours and you know what the airport traffic is like."

"But Mom…"

"Don't but-mom me. Do as you're told and get up those stairs."

One look at her mother's face warned Susan not to say anything more. All she'd wanted to know was... But what did it matter? Anywhere was better than home right now. She started up the stairs.

"And remember to wash your hair. You have beautiful hair, you know, and you need to take care of it. You don't know how lucky you are. I only wish I had gorgeous hair like yours."

"Well, you can have it," muttered Susan. She considered cutting it all off and throwing it at her. She hated her long hair. Her father had told her to get it buzzed if she wanted, but her mother insisted that it remain long, because that was more 'feminine.'

When Susan walked damply out of the steamed-up bathroom and into her bedroom, one towel wrapped around her hair and another around her body, she found a green T-shirt, a pair of jeans and her new tennis shoes laid out.

"What...?" She swept them to the floor. "How dare she." Susan stepped on the pile. She always chose her own clothes. Then she reconsidered. She'd had enough of fighting with her mother for one day and since she was leaving anyway, maybe she could yield on this point. But when she picked up her Tee-shirt, she saw it was too wet and wrinkled to put on. Besides, she wanted to wear her red one. She threw the green one under the bed and dressed.

Susan glanced in the mirror at her tangled mess of

hair. "Beautiful, indeed!" She stuck her tongue out at her reflection. Snatching up a comb, she dragged it through the shoulder-length rat's nest and headed downstairs, continuing to comb her hair and creating a collar of water drips on her shirt. On the last step, she stopped, comb in mid-stroke.

Her mother sat primly in the dining room, perfectly dressed as always, looking like she'd stepped out of *Southern Living* magazine, car keys jingling in her hand. Susan's suitcase stood at attention beside her, its pull handle fully extended, ready to go. The book on Queen Elizabeth I lay on her suitcase. On top of the book perched a ziploc bag of chocolate chip cookies.

"You packed for me?"

"Yes." Mrs. Cardiff stood up, brushing nonexistent crumbs from her lap. "You know I hate delays."

"Where am I going?"

Mrs. Cardiff seemed not to hear. She was already in motion, leaving Susan to tug the suitcase behind her, scrambling to catch up. When they were in the car, seatbelts fastened, doors locked, accelerating towards the airport, she asked about her destination again.

This time her mother replied. "Aunt Camellia's."

"What!"

"For two weeks. Longer if you wish, which might not be a bad idea, given what I have to sort out with your father."

"But…"

"It's high time you and your aunt met and she got to know you."

The shock of actually spending time with the great and mysterious Aunt Camellia vied with curiosity in Susan's mind. "Where does she live?"

"North Carolina."——

Susan rolled her eyes. She already knew that. "*Where* in North Carolina?"

"Carolina Beach. It'll be lovely to be at a real beach, not like the rocky things here in Maine." This was a sore point with Mrs. Cardiff. She was positive that any number of colleges in the South would be only too happy to have her husband teach Classics, and she simply could not understand why they had to stay in New England. Even his artistic Aunt Camellia lived in the South. "I almost wish I were going instead," she said.

24

"Is Carolina Beach where the candy stripe light-house is?"

"That's Cape Hatteras."

"Where's Carolina Beach?"

"In the southeastern part, near Wilmington."

"Southeastern North Carolina," muttered Susan. "Too many directions for one place."

"'By indirection find direction out,'" quoted Mrs. Cardiff.

"That's Shakespeare," Susan said, stealing a side-long glance at her mother. "Look." She took her book on Queen Elizabeth, flipped to the epigraph to confirm the quotation came from *Hamlet*, then went back to the cover. "And it's in the title. See." Her finger underlined the words—*By Indirection*.

"Hmm."

She'd never heard her mother display any knowl-edge of the art and literature that were part of her father's world. Who was this woman her father said had once been a balance of efficiency and tenderness? Where had she gone? Susan wondered if she'd ever know.

Her mother lit a cigarette and concentrated on smoking and driving, saying nothing more to Susan, who waited for the conversation to continue. When it didn't, she looked at the book Aunt Camellia had sent her and thought about her aunt. She recalled the conversation she'd had with her father last year.

"What's Aunt Camellia like, Papa?"

"Well, she's…majestic. No, regal describes her better, one of those women who are queens of themselves. You'll see when you meet her one day."

"And she's rich."

"Which she didn't inherit because no one on my side of the family was ever rich, at least as far as I know. But we Welsh have a strange lot of ancestors whose connections with things marvelous, mystic and magical never stay locked in the past. That's why there's a dragon on the Welsh flag—to remind us. And there's something more than natural in Camellia's art, though what I've never quite been able to put my finger on. It's a bit like trying to see something in a fog—just when you think you see a boat or a buoy, thicker fog billows around it and the thing is gone before you can really say it was there. It's as if she's been somewhere marvelous and come back laden with true treasures—experiences, memories, knowledge, wisdom, and beauties, like the carpet. And now she paints scenes of it and speaks in riddles and lavishes her attention on you. I've always been grateful that she likes me, and I don't think you can imagine how happy I am that she likes you more than she does any of her other relatives. I know it's bad parenting to live through your child, but in your case I do. And I confess I'm a little envious of all she does for you—I certainly never got such gifts. Even though I know she loves me more than any of my cousins, the boys especially, there's never been the sort of connection she feels with you, Sue C. Did you know the painting you like so much is by her?"

"Aunt Camellia did that?" For Susan, the large painting had always seemed to be a view seen by someone standing partway up a mountain. The first time she'd seen it, she'd felt a curious tingling. One day she'd borrowed her father's binoculars and tried to see further into the painting but couldn't quite get them focused.

"She painted it for you in fact. It's yours."

"Mine? Can I have it in my room?"

27

"I don't think that'd be a good idea. Your mother doesn't want you to have it until you're older, so she's sort of keeping it for you in the living room."

"So she can brag about it."

"I think she might say to share it with visitors."

"Do *you* like Aunt Camellia's paintings, Papa?

"Goodness, yes! I think they're fabulous."

"Then I don't mind my painting hanging in the living room where you can see it whenever you want."

Her father smiled. "And the magic flying Persian carpet, which isn't Persian at all..."

"Is mine, too?"

Her father nodded. "And so brilliantly made and of such a unique design that my friend Ahmed—you remember, he's the short bald one with the black moustache—well, he offered me a queen's ransom for it. I told him it was yours and he didn't have my permission to discuss it with you because you're a minor. But you can count on his showing up when you're twenty-one to repeat his offer, you just watch."

"I'll never sell it—it's too beautiful. Are you sure it's really mine?"

28

"Aunt Camellia told me so. She made me stipulate it in an addition to my will."

"She doesn't trust Mommy." Susan remembered her mother's hostility on the day of the carpet's arrival. "Mommy wouldn't even let me see the paper the delivery men brought. I bet my name was on it, not hers."

"Well, ah…" Her father cleared his throat. "Enough said on that matter, I think."

Susan had burned with indignation. The thought of her mother's furniture marring her carpet made her want to get an axe and chop up the ridiculous French provincial coffee table, especially its pointed feet. She turned her angry face up to her father, but his sad look evaporated her desire for revenge. Poor Papa. She decided to talk about something more pleasant.

"Why does she make me make me learn so much?"

"Who?"

"Aunt Camellia."

"I'm not sure, but she took such an interest in you that she told me what we should call you."

"Aunt Camellia named me?"

Her father suddenly looked guilty. "No, of course

not. I mean, not exactly. That is…"

"Pa-pa…" She dragged out both syllables, wheedling a more complete answer.

"Well, the truth is she phoned when Mommy was pregnant with you—in fact, on the same day we got the news from the doctor—and she simply told me in that way of hers that your name had to be Camellia. That was fine with me because I was thinking the same thing if you turned out to be a girl. And things might've been okay if I hadn't told your mother. But I did and…well, she said she'd just see about that. So when you did turn out to be a girl, Mommy said your name was Susan, which was fine with me because I liked that name too. Then when I filled out the papers for your birth certificate, I…I couldn't refuse Aunt Camellia, could I, so it turned out you got both names–Susan Camellia. And I've sort of run both of them together, haven't I, my Sue C.?"

"But how did Aunt Camellia know I was a girl?"

Her father had shrugged his shoulders. "I never told anybody else about it—till now. But your mother did. And before I knew it, those silly relatives of mine were filling her ears with all kinds of stories about Aunt

30

C. being a witch and—"

"Aunt Camellia's a witch?"

"Of course not. She's...herself. And rich enough to do what she wants no matter what my cousins say. But then she always did anyway, as far as I can tell. I don't think wealth has a thing to do with who Aunt Camellia is or why she does what she does. I'm of the opinion that wealth is her disguise. You'll understand when you meet her. When she heard she was being called a witch, I believe she quite liked it. She's never done a thing to dissuade people of the idea. Helped keep stupid people away, she told me once."

Mrs. Cardiff broke into Susan's recollection.

"I want you to promise not to get into trouble while you're there—you know what I mean. And finish reading that book on the plane—your aunt's bound to ask you a hundred questions about it, and you want to start out on the right foot."

Susan nodded her head and pretended to read. The sigh she forced through her nose fluttered the pages. Two more weeks without Papa. And with a strange, rich woman who was probably a witch. Great.

CHAPTER THREE

CAROLINA

"This is the captain speaking."

Susan stared out the airplane window, legs tucked under her, pleased that rich Aunt Camellia had bought her a first-class ticket.

"We'll be landing shortly in Wilmington, ladies and gentlemen, the heart of southeastern North Carolina, home of the Confederate blockade runners, major port of the Cape Fear River..."

Susan pushed her face against the window glass. She'd read about Cape Fear in her book on Queen Elizabeth. The English had made their first settlement in America somewhere near here back in the queen's time—the 1500s.

She was disappointed with Wilmington airport's lack of even a smidgen of history—no English flag, no paintings of Queen Elizabeth or of blockade runners. She might as well be in Kansas as Carolina. And having to be escorted off the plane to the terminal! So what if the airline rules said an underage child unaccompanied by an adult had to have a stewardess take her on and off the flight. How was it okay for her to canoe in Labrador but not to walk off a commercial airliner? Worst of all was her discovery that the stewardess wouldn't leave until whoever was meeting Susan showed up.

"I can wait by myself, I'm not helpless."

"Look, dearie, the rules say I have to stay with you until your party shows up." The stewardess took out a cigarette, broke off the filter and lit it.

"I could get cancer from your secondhand smoke, you know."

Removing the cigarette from her lips, the stewardess blew out a blue stream of smoke. With two blood-red, pincer-like fingernails, she plucked a thread of tobacco from the tip of her tongue and flicked it in Susan's direction.

The sudden rush of angry heat that swept over Susan dried up her vocabulary. She heard herself panting like one of those angry bulls on the travel channel.

The stewardess, however, had both words and voice:

"Your father, dearie."

Susan stared at the fingernail's target. From an unframed canvas held by a pair of rough and callused hands stared a portrait of Susan, rendered in a few brilliant strokes of red. Emblazoned in dark, clear letters was her name: *S. Camellia Cardiff.* An old man barely Susan's height held the painting. His gaunt face, melancholy eyes drooping sadly at their corners, hovered above it. One of his gnarled hands clasped each side of the painting, and a pair of short legs draped in baggy-kneed khaki trousers seemed to grow down from the bottom of it. Susan stole an embarrassed glance in the stewardess's direction, relieved to see the woman walking away, smoke trailing behind her.

Still simmering from the stewardess's haughty dismissal, Susan turned her attention to the little old man and his sign. She marched up to him. "Did Aunt Camellia send you?"

He removed a work-rough hand from the sign and plucked an imaginary cap from his head of white hair. "Yes'm."

"My name's **SUSAN**!" She stamped her foot in

punctuation. "I'm *not* Camellia and I'll never *be* Camellia!"

The old fellow blinked but seemed unaffected by either her words or the vitriol behind them. "This way to the car, please. I'll tend to your bags."

Without waiting to see if she followed him, Aunt Camellia's man headed towards the exit. Susan ran to catch up, bursting out of the air-conditioned terminal into a blanket of hot and humid Carolina air. She gasped, not at the sultry air but at her aunt's car—a silvery-green Rolls Royce convertible. Papa's friend who wanted to buy her carpet had one too, but it was a sickly yellow.

The little man held the rear door open for her. She slipped in and sprawled luxuriously, feeling the eyes of the twenty or so nearby people on her. What was a little humid weather when she rode through it in a Rolls? Like a queen! She twisted round to see if she could catch a glimpse of the stewardess and make the rude woman look at her now. No such luck.

Susan smiled when the little man removed his cap and put on a chauffeur's hat. Nothing disturbed her sense of well-being on the drive to her aunt's. Not the whiff of foul air from the sewage treatment ponds at the end of the airport driveway. Not the sight of rusty oil storage tanks blocking the view of the Cape Fear River when they left old Wilmington and its historic homes along tree-shaded streets. Not the miles of strip malls, golf ranges, suburbs behind gates bearing silly names. Not the trailer parks or fast-food franchises that looked like Anywhere USA. Susan scarcely saw any of it as the rumpled chauffeur directed the Rolls on prairie-flat roads to Carolina Beach. Snow's Cut Bridge seemed to arch itself in surprise as they left the mainland. From the apex of the bridge Susan saw the great green Atlantic Ocean a mile away.

"Intracoastal Waterway," shouted Aunt Camellia's man, gesturing left and right at the stretch of water under the bridge.

Just before the car headed down the other side of the bridge, Susan noticed a large point of land on the ocean side, empty of buildings except for one large and vaguely familiar house. Then the view was gone as the car dipped earthward into Carolina Beach. A bulbous water tower proclaimed the town's name.

Carolina Beach. A waterslide park guarded by a discolored and disintegrating dinosaur. Gas stations. Restaurants and motels. A left turn at the marina full of shrimp boats, sport fishing boats, yachts, and huge party boats. Left again at the lights. Admiring glances from tourists. Then many motels, even more condos, and a few small, original beach cottages looking out of place.

The road eventually ended at an antique iron gate in a cinderblock wall. The car slowed, the gate swung silently open, and as the Rolls drove through Susan saw the words *Beware Witch* crudely sprayed in red paint on the wall. The gate closed silently and eerily behind her.

Susan felt prepared to find anything behind the brick wall—a wasteland of broken concrete with bits of rusty steel rod poking through, or a barren stretch of smoldering grass leading to a black and sinister castle, or a dusty, treeless plain patrolled by savage dogs. But the calm beauty of the natural Carolina landscape was a surprise. She sat in admiring silence until they'd passed the last of the trees and the remaining acres of her aunt's estate lay open to the sky, with splendid vistas of the waterway on one side and a tidal marsh, sand dunes, and the sea beyond on the other. Then the large, solitary house snared Susan's complete attention.

"A Tudor mansion! *Incroyable!*" Incredible.

Susan leafed through her book, wanting to find the photograph her aunt's house reminded her of. Where *was* it? Not there, not there... But she'd *seen* it...ah, *there*. Her eyes flicked from photo to mansion and back again. Except for the Carolina setting, she could see no difference between the two.

The mansion looked so genuinely *old*, not like the plastic artificiality of a Disney imitation. The diamond panes of the windows reflected light at different angles, which Susan knew meant each little pane was a separate piece of glass. Modern houses achieved the Tudor effect by gluing a plastic stencil of diamond shapes to a single pane of window glass. It was fast and easy, Papa had explained, but, as far as he was concerned, it was another blow to Beauty, one more example of the Disneyfication of the world.

"There's always a cost to Beauty," he had said, emphasizing the capital B. "But if you want the Real Thing, you've got to pay—time, effort, money, something."

Susan was positive her aunt's house was a Real Thing. Not just the diamond-paned windows said it, but the splits in the oak timbers, the thickness of the cracked stucco with gaps where pieces had fallen off did too. The way which sections of the house seemed to slouch from fatigue said it as well. Most of all, the coat-of-arms on the ancient plaque over the front door said it.

Susan looked from the coat-of-arms over her aunt's door to the one over the door of the mansion in the photograph. They seemed identical. Two heraldic beasts—one a dragon, the other a lion that looked like a shaggy dog with a bad haircut—stood on their hind legs holding a circle with a flower in it. Susan knew it was the Tudor rose but it seemed to her more like, well, a camellia. Resting on the circle, and at eye level with the dragon and the lion, was a crown that had a square cross on its highest point. The cross separated two large initials: E R—Elizabeth Rex—Queen Elizabeth.

How had her aunt done it? How had she acquired the mansion of Queen Elizabeth and got it here in the southeastern corner of North Carolina? The spray-painted words flashed in her mind: *Beware Witch.*

CHAPTER FOUR

THE MAILBOX

"Darling!"

Susan instantly liked Aunt Camellia. She looked neither young nor old, just tall and fit, her long white hair twisted into a loose bun kept in place by an artist's paintbrush. She wore tennis shoes, blue jeans rolled up to mid-calf, and an untucked blouse. Elegant black eyebrows arched over the same deep brown eyes Susan had. This was no witch.

"I was beginning to wonder if you'd ever arrive. Where *did* Dinkins drive you?" Susan scrambled out of the Rolls into her aunt's open arms. "But never mind right now. Take her things to her room, Dinkins, there's a good man. And send Scruggs out, would you."

Dinkins bowed. "Yes, you maj—"

Susan felt her aunt stiffen. She twisted round to witness Dinkins cover his mouth and cough. "Yes'm.

Right away."

Susan wondered at the interchange between Dinkins and her aunt. Papa had said she was regal and that most of her relatives thought she was weird. Was this an example of both? Maybe Aunt Camellia had her servants call her 'Your Majesty' when no one was around.

Aunt Camellia kissed the top of Susan's head. "I know you'll adore your room, but why don't we find ourselves a comfortable corner and get to know one another? We've hardly seen one another in all these years."

"I'd like that, Aunt Camellia."

Dinkins' female counterpart appeared in the front doorway.

"Ah, Scruggs. Bring a pot of mint tea and a plate of cucumber sandwiches to the Great Hall, there's a dear."

"Yes'm." Scruggs made a low curtsey.

"Now, my darling niece, you must tell me what you think of this quaint part of the world and what artifact that papa of yours is constructing *this* summer."

But before Susan could respond, Aunt Camellia rushed on. "Well, darling, your impressions?"

They stood in the doorway of a huge room. Aunt

Camellia gestured with the hand of her free arm, as if she'd conjured the room into existence that very moment. "The Great Hall." Her movement sparked a flash of green from the huge emerald on her finger. Susan's eye followed the light's quick path across the hall.

As far as Susan could tell, the Great Hall ran the length of the house. It certainly went to the roof. She could see the steep angle of the roofline beyond the crossbeams above her. Three iron chandeliers filled with unlighted candles dangled on long chains from the beams.

"It must look glorious when there's a party and they're all alight with people dancing beneath." Susan spun in a circle, imagining herself in a red velvet gown with strings of pearls and bracelets of gold glinting and jangling on her bare arms. Maybe it was her twenty-first birthday. She stopped suddenly, imagining her mother frowning at her, but the only one watching was Aunt Camellia. And she was smiling.

"Yes, the parties *are* wonderful."

Of course such an aunt would understand. Susan spun herself once more and caught sight of the massive fireplace at the end of the hall. "You could burn whole trees in there."

Up close the fireplace seemed even bigger. She walked into it and raised her arms above her head. Balancing on her toes, she was able to brush the top with her fingers. Amazing! She stared up the long, black tunnel of a chimney and saw a small patch of blue sky that looked miles away. A strange desire to walk to the end of the chimney-tunnel came over her. Then a horrible thought flitted into her mind: not only trees could burn in there. She hopped out of the cavernous fireplace and wiped her sooty fingertips on her jeans.

Susan was going to tell Aunt Camellia about her curious desire to walk out the chimney when she was distracted by a gigantic gold shield over the doorway her aunt stood in. She knew it was a Real Thing. The gold gleamed in the sunlight pouring on it from the windows. She tingled as she gazed at the giant shield, mesmerized.

Aunt Camellia observed Susan closely. "What do you see?"

Susan spoke as if she were in a trance. "It's like a map and a movie at the same time. When I look at one spot, that place takes over the whole map. It's what I always wanted to happen with the landscape you painted for me. I'm looking at the tall mountains, and there's a crater with a waterfall so high the water is mist by the time it reaches the little lake at the bottom. A zigzag road goes up from the lake to the top of the waterfall. And in the sky—an incredible star! The sky's turning into a gold wall filled with jewels and lines are connecting them, making a…"

"Enough!" commanded Aunt Camellia. "Look at me!" Her voice echoed in the hall, rattling the windowpanes.

Susan heard only a whisper. Blinking heavy eyes, she slowly turned her face towards her aunt. "You called me, Your Majesty?" Her words were thick with dream.

"Yes, my darling." Aunt Camellia guided her out of the Great Hall to a sitting room and sat her in a large chair.

"Here's Scruggs with mint tea and cucumber sandwiches. Eat, sweetie. The seeds are quite small and Scruggs made the bread this morning."

Because she kept forgetting what she was doing, Susan needed a long time to finish the first sandwich.

"Take another bite, darling," Aunt Camellia urged. The second sandwich took less time to eat and the third even less. With every sandwich she ate, Susan regained more of herself. At last the plate held only crumbs, and the teapot soggy tea leaves. Susan, however, felt restless with energy.

"Why don't you explore the beach?" Aunt Camellia suggested. "Scruggs assures me we have hours before dinner. If I didn't have a painting I really must put the finishing touches to, we could go swimming. After dinner, perhaps. There's a footbridge over the salt marsh that takes you right to the shore. Just ask Dinkins to point it out."

Running along the beach and splashing in the waves was something she'd looked forward to on the flight. "As long as you promise you'll go swimming later."

"I promise. Now give me a kiss before you go."

Susan ran the length of the bridge and fell breathless on the crest of the first sand dune. The sea oats swayed in the wind and squadrons of pelicans skimmed the breaking waves. "Wow! The whole place to myself." The beach was deserted.

She took off her tennis shoes and left them on the dune. Wishing her mother had set out shorts to wear instead of jeans, she rolled up the legs to mid-calf, just like Aunt Camellia's, and headed for the water. At first, she enjoyed the feel of the hard sand and warm water on her feet and the discovery of so many unbroken shells, but an uneasiness prodded her to return. When she reached the dunes with her pockets full of shells, she didn't see her shoes. "I know I left them here," she said.

A black-headed gull floated above her, laughing.

"Easy for you—you don't have shoes and mine were brand new."

The gull wheeled away with a parting laugh.

She stumbled on them closer to the bridge. Stuffing the socks in her back pockets, she tried to put her feet into the sneakers.

"Ow!" The sand sticking to her feet scratched her painfully. As she pulled her socks out of her pockets, the wind snatched one and tumbled it over the dune. "Stop!" she shouted, chasing it down. Balancing on one leg, she brushed the sand from her foot, slipped on the sock and put on her shoe. Her hair, tangled from wind and salt, fell in her eyes. When she pushed it back, she felt the sand from her hands stick to it, adding to the mess. "Aargh! If I had scissors…"

She grabbed a fistful of hair and mimicked her mother: "'You have such beautiful hair.' Well, mother dear, I wish it was all cut off and put in a bag just for you!"

She made her way towards the footbridge, rehearsing scene after scene in which she got the better of her mother over the issue of her 'beautiful hair.' She was particularly enjoying one confrontation in which her mother had to cook and eat it when she reached the bridge and was startled to see a mailbox standing beside it. "Where'd *you* come from?" She was positive there hadn't been a mailbox there when she first crossed the bridge.

Going up to it, she grasped the small round handle of its door and tugged. It didn't move. With her other hand she grabbed the hand that held the handle and tugged again. The tiniest of rusty movements. Inhaling deeply, she pulled again. "Stupid…thing," she grunted, her arms fully extended, head back, her body leaning away from the mailbox.

Just when it seemed the flimsy handle would likely break, the door gave way, tearing at her ears with a hideous groan. She lost her balance and fell. From the sand she glared up at the broken door. It hung from the one hinge that had survived her assault.

"Serves you right," she said, getting up and brushing off the sand. She bent over and looked in.

It was like staring up the tunnel of Aunt Camellia's chimney—but instead of a patch of blue, a tiny circle of gold punctuated the long darkness. She moved her head aside and reached in, looking for treasure. In Elizabeth's time, Cape Fear had been famous for pirates. Could there be a Spanish doubloon in this old mailbox?

Although her fingers were able to touch the sides and bottom, they couldn't reach the end of the mailbox where the gold beckoned. She pulled out her arm and looked in again. Yes, the gold circle still shone at the back. Susan went to the side of the mailbox and measured her arm against it. Her arm was longer. Why couldn't it reach the back, then? She hated things that didn't make sense.

"All right, mailbox, enough is enough."

Susan stepped up to the dark opening and put both of her arms in, wedging her elbows against the inner sides of the mailbox. Perfect. She'd learned this trick at rock-climbing camp. Climbers used it to pull themselves through narrow openings that provided no handholds or footholds. She put her head between her arms, pushed with her legs, pulled with her arms, and heaved herself into the mailbox. Only her legs stuck out. One more pull and a vigorous wriggle delivered her into the mailbox. But she still could not reach the end where the gold gleamed.

Then a marvelous thought struck her. Her aunt really *was* a witch, and this was a shortcut back to the mansion. That's why her aunt had sent her to the beach—to find the mailbox tunnel! The gold at the end of the tunnel was really the reflection from the gold shield in the hall. Wouldn't Aunt Camellia be surprised when she re-appeared in the house?

Susan discovered that the top of the mailbox was higher than she thought—high enough to allow her to get on her hands and knees and crawl towards the shield. She chuckled to herself at the thought of arriving just in time for dinner through the magic tunnel, which must end in the giant fireplace. The further Susan went, the brighter the golden light grew. The tunnel had now become high enough for her to stand up without bumping her head.

As she walked on, the golden light grew so bright she had to squint. When she reached the end of the tunnel, she found herself standing on a smooth floor. She didn't recall the bottom of her aunt's fireplace feeling like the marble floor of St. Peter's Cathedral, which she'd visited with Papa last Easter. But what did it matter, she shrugged, she'd got back through the secret tunnel.

"Aunt Camellia, I'm here! I found the tunnel!"

"Tunnel…tunnel…tunnel…" Her words echoed emptily and ever more faintly as if she were standing in a mountain pass. Susan shivered. Something was very wrong.

CHAPTER FIVE

GYLDFEN

Susan stared at her frightened reflection in the polished floor, then raised her eyes. Awe momentarily drove out her fright. Where *is* this? she wondered, gawking at a golden-walled cavern as vast as a cathedral. Trying to see it all, she turned in a circle, stopping when she faced the entrance of the mailbox tunnel. Immediately, she felt secure. She could leave anytime she wanted. Maybe she'd explore the cavern a little first. On the wall that soared above the tunnel entrance, sparks of color seemed to wink at her. "They're jewels!" she blurted.

"Jewels!…jewels!…jewels!" mocked the great golden cavern.

Susan froze. The fading words raised goosebumps on her arms. When she realized she was holding her breath, she imitated her karate sensei: "Breathe!"

"Breathe!…breathe!…breathe!…"

She tensed at the echo and held her breath again,

then relaxed and followed her own instruction. When she looked up at the jewels again, Susan noticed hundreds more. It was as if they were colored stars coming out after sunset in a golden sky. She scanned them for constellations but, unable to recognize any, she decided she'd make her own. She had enough stars. Where to start?

An emerald as large as the one in Aunt Camellia's ring and a nearby ruby looked promising. Susan blinked in surprise. Lines had suddenly appeared, curving around the two jewels to engrave a crocodile face. Then the lines raced away from the face, engraving a huge reptilian body with long legs, each tipped with claws of small rubies. Magnificent wings sprouted from the creature's back and a tapering tail snaked its way down to a diamond finale. Seeing the bejeweled golden dragon spring into existence was like watching an artist paint a cartoon character who then gave orders to its creator. She refused to believe she'd had anything to do with the appearance of the dragon on the wall in front of her. "You're not real!"

"Real!…real!…real!" contradicted the cavern.

She turned her back on the engraving, crossed her arms and wished she were back in Aunt Camellia's house. "Stupid mailbox," she whispered under her breath, careful not to set off the echoes. "I wish I'd never found it. I never asked to be here, and it's not my fault I made a dragon."

But Susan couldn't shake off the feeling that, somehow, it was her fault, at least partly. And worse, she imagined the dragon coming alive on the wall behind her. "Stop it!" she cried to her uncontrollable imagination, and then to the dragon alive in her mind: "You can't live!"

"…live!…live!…live!" countered her echo.

Susan shivered in sudden fear. She wanted to run away, get out of the cavern that instant. But not through the mailbox tunnel. No, she shuddered, not that way. She couldn't turn around and look at the dragon, which she'd have to do, because the tunnel entrance lay between the creature's legs. It wasn't fair that her escape was through the dragon. "That can't be the only way."

"…only way…only way," insisted the echoing cavern.

So Susan set out in search of another exit. Behind her, two puffs of smoke broke from the dragon's nostrils and floated lazily up the wall. She wandered aimlessly in the golden emptiness, going nowhere and finding nothing. "This is pointless," she muttered. "You already know where there's an exit." When she realized she'd gone in a circle, her eyes welled with tears. "But I can't look at that thing, I can't. It's scary."

"…scary…scary…scary," the echo confirmed.

Susan collapsed on the floor and began to cry, lying face down, weeping into her arms. She'd never felt more miserable. At last, she rolled onto her back and raised her hand to wipe away the stinging tears. She stared at her hand—it was black with grime! She glanced at her clothes and saw the same filth covering them. It was as if she'd been dragged through a black and greasy chimney. When she pulled a handful of her hair in front of her eyes, she found it too was begrimed with the sooty stuff. How had it happened?

"Welcome to the Gold Hall of Gylla," a voice purred, setting the cavern echoing and making Susan's skin crawl.

Instantly, she was on her feet. "Who said that?" She scanned the hall, seeking the speaker, and found the dragon's eyes contemplating her from the wall. Staring into them, Susan felt powerless to look anywhere else. Instead of carrying her away, her feet seemed to root her to the polished floor.

"Welcome to Ebal," the velvet-voiced dragon added.

Susan stared at the monster swelling and bulging from the wall. Gold smoke belched from its nostrils. The mouth gaped, displaying a fence of jagged teeth. Looking like a rope of scorched meat, the long tongue slid out, split at the end. As the tongue's quivering tips hissed towards her face, licking the air around her, she whimpered. Terrified, she watched the bulging dragon stretch its legs, cat-like, from the wall and rest them on the floor. Its smooth body changed to a shimmering mass of golden scales. The open wings folded themselves. Only the tail's diamond tip tethered the dragon to the wall. When it turned its head to witness its liberation, Susan suddenly felt free and able to move her feet.

A bearded little man, shorter than Susan and dressed all in green—shapeless green hat, baggy green peacoat, baggy green trousers—dashed out from a passageway she hadn't seen and grabbed her.

"Quick!" he panted. "This way!"

They scampered across the cavern towards the passageway. A few short feet inside it, he turned to shut a stone door behind them. Susan slumped to the floor, exhausted.

She felt the rush of hot air before she heard the dragon's roar or saw the flames play around the closing door. When one tiny tongue scorched her leg, she leapt up and helped shut the door, then slid back to the floor, relieved. Her rescuer rooted in a leather shoulder bag he carried and pulled out a large stone key, repeatedly jabbing it at the blank wall of the door.

"It's here somewhere," the little man muttered. "I know it is—at least, it's supposed to be. I'm sure this is the right Gate."

To Susan's surprise, a keyhole appeared after one of his jabs and he inserted the key, but he couldn't turn it completely in the lock. He pushed against the door, trying to move it the tiny distance he needed to lock it. He tried the key again. No luck. He cast a desperate look at her.

"If you could just…"

She pushed against the door with all her strength while he strained to twist the key.

"More!" he grunted.

Susan planted her heels, bent her legs, and thrust.

"Pressure…" he explained, "…of Gyldfen's fire…stopping…door…," his face turned scarlet with his heroic last effort, "…closing!" The door moved and the key turned.

"There." He withdrew the key and patted the stone door. "No dragon can open that Gate or even find it now."

Susan watched the outline of the door vanish, leaving only a seamless stone wall. "Where'd it go?"

"It's still there, but '*Without the key, there's naught to see.*' And it's exactly the same on the other side—nothing to be seen. I hope Gyldfen burns himself to cinders trying to blast the wall with his fire." The little man chuckled as he dropped the key into his capacious bag.

"We best be going, Your Majesty."

He took a few steps down the passage, stopped suddenly and scurried back, sheepishly pulling off his shapeless green hat. He bowed very low, which caused his shoulder bag to slide onto his neck and overbalance him, dropping both man and bag to the floor.

"I beg your most humble pardon, Your Majesty," he said, twisting his head to look up at Susan. "I mean, I *humbly* beg…that is, Jon o'Gates, *humbly*, is at your humble service."

Susan laughed and, reaching a hand down to her rescuer, helped him up.

"I'm terribly sorry I'm so late, Your Majesty, but it's been so many years, you see, and you didn't come and then I made the journey here with my father purposely to receive the key, you understand,"—he touched his bag, indicating the key he mentioned rested in it—"just as he'd made the journey with his father when he was a young man—my father, I mean—and his father before him and on and on into the past, almost forever. And then—like a miracle!—I dreamed the dream only the Giver can send, but it'd been so long, you see, and my father was dead and I wasn't really a young man anymore and I wasn't sure if was a *real* dream, *the* dream, the one that all the Keepers of the Gates dream about dreaming but so few do, and here I was dreaming it, which no one thought would ever happen because I…well, you see, some people just don't think I'm a fit Keeper, Your Majesty, and so how could I tell if I weren't making up the dream just so I, Jon o'Gates, could be *the* Keeper to do it and show all those mockers? Anyway, because of all that, I didn't start out for the Gates *immediately*, which I should've done as soon as the dream was dreamed— oh, Your Majesty, such a dream!—nor did I walk as fast as I should have after receiving the dream, but when I saw those puffs of golden smoke rise from the mountain, then I *knew* the dream was true and I really *was* the one to let you in but I didn't have wings to get me here in time and how I feared my legs would never carry me up the mountain and when they did and I saw how Gyldfen was about to enslave you, Your Majesty, I just wanted to die I was so ashamed because where would we all be if that happened?—you being Gyldfen's slave, I mean— and it would've happened because I let the mockers make me doubt I was a Keeper of the Gates, and so I didn't go to check the Gates every year as my father had and his father and on and on because I didn't believe enough and look what trouble I had trying to open and close just *one* Gate—but I *did* open a Gate, didn't I? And here you are just like the Histories said."

Susan took Jon's square hands in hers and looked into his bright blue eyes. "Thank you, Jon o'Gates, for rescuing me—only a hero could've done it. I wish I had something to reward you with."

"Your most gracious majesty…"

"However, I am *not* your queen. So, if you'll just show me the way out, I'll get going and you can wait until the real queen shows up."

"But only the queen can enter Ebal through the Gold Hall of Mt. Gylla! It's all written down in the Histories. There's *never* a mistake!"

"Well, there is this time, because I am not the queen. I'm not even from here."

"None of the queens are. That's why there are Gates and a Keeper of the Gates. We dream the dream of the queen and then go to the Gates and open them with the key. If you weren't the queen, I wouldn't have dreamed you and you wouldn't be here and I wouldn't have let you in. But I did, so you must be the queen."

"Look, you silly little man! I was visiting my Aunt Camellia and was just coming back from the beach when a stupid mailbox popped up out of nowhere and I climbed in it…" She shook away the gate-like image of the mailbox's rusty door hanging by a single hinge. Then memories of Dinkins calling her aunt 'Your Majesty' and her father calling her 'queenly' rose in her mind. Had her aunt once been Queen of Ebal? No, that couldn't be possible.

"Niece to Queen Camellia the Green! Just as the Histories say. There's no mistake. You're the new Queen Camellia."

It was one thing to read about Queen Elizabeth and feel queenly riding in a Rolls Royce. It was quite another to be declared a queen by a clumsy, talkative little man after ending up in a dragon's lair. It was just too much. "My name's not Camellia."

Jon stepped back in surprise. "Your name's *not* Camellia?"

"No. My name's Susan."

"Susan," repeated Jon o'Gates, "not Camellia. How could there be a mistake?" he muttered. "I know she's covered in black, which wasn't in the dream, but she still looks like the queen I dreamed, and maybe her first gate was dirty. Oh, I wish I'd studied the Histories more! Poor Father tried to make me because he said a dangerous and confusing time for one of the Keepers was coming and I needed to learn about it in case I was that Keeper, but I said no queen had come for ages and ages, so why would one come now? And if she did my father could open the Gates and know what to do. So I went exploring my beautiful Ebal and didn't read thick old books with tiny words in tiny letters—not when Ebal called me to come find it. And then Father died and no queen had come and then I was the Keeper of the Gates and maybe I would've read more of the Histories but Piotr was always so angry when I went to him to help me and he'd never take a break or go rambling so I studied even less and look what's happened! I'm a useless Keeper who doesn't know anything because…"

He stopped and looked at Susan.

"If you're not a queen…?"

Susan admitted to herself that she liked the idea of being queen of somewhere, especially after the way her mother mistreated her. And here was a chance to be a queen—even though it would be by mistake. But what a mess—dragons and gates and prophecies and the right name and coronations (what sort of crown did the queen wear, she wondered). And *she* was a filthy mess with no idea of how to get clean. And then there was poor Jon o'Gates. The only way to help him seemed to be to admit that Camellia was not only one of her names but also the one both her aunt and her father had selected. Feeling guilty about something she could do to help but didn't want to do made her angry. What was she to Ebal or Ebal to her that she should be queen of it?

"Can't you open the Gate and let me go back to my aunt's?"

"But Gyldfen is loose!"

"You mean he's still in there?"

Jon nodded.

Susan had hoped the dragon had melted back into the golden wall. "Can't you call someone to get rid of him?"

"That's the queen's duty, at least according to the Histories."

"What!"

"Camellia the Green did it last time by carving him into the wall somehow. I'm pretty sure that whoever frees him has to bind him, but if you're not the queen, and you've loosed Gyldfen, then who...?"

Susan despaired of a solution. No way out and a dragon she apparently was responsible for.

"I can't take you to Ingersoll, " Jon lamented.

"No," Susan agreed, "you can't."

Wherever Ingersoll was, it had something to do with being queen. And she wasn't going down that road. But she had to go somewhere to find a way back. She needed to think. If she could put the dragon out of her mind for a few minutes, then maybe she could... Susan dropped into lotus. She settled her breathing and gradually calmed her mind long enough to get a perfectly obvious idea.

"You say you've traveled a lot in Ebal, right?" she asked.

"Yes, Your Majesty, more than most, although..."

"So you've met a lot of people?"

"Not just people, Your Majesty! In the Forest of…"

"We don't have time for that now."

"Yes, Your Majesty."

"Among all the…acquaintances you've encountered, who has the most knowledge of Ebal?"

"Why didn't I think of that?"

"Who is it?"

"Why Piotr, of course. He taught my father and his father and maybe his. He's very old, Your Majesty, and there are stories that…"

"I command you to stop talking and take me to Piotr!"

"Yes, Your Majesty."

"Good. But stop calling me 'Your Majesty'."

"But…"

Susan had worked it out in her mind. "You can call me Sue C."

"Souci?"

"What did you say?" He'd pronounced it as a French word, *souci*, which meant 'gentle.' She wondered what her father would think of it—Susan and Camellia combined to make Gentle.

"Didn't I say it right, Your Majesty?"

"Yes, Jon, perfectly. Let's go to your Piotr."

Jon led Susan out of the passageway. The smell of fresh air lifted her spirit. She wasn't sure what she'd been expecting when she stepped onto the mountain ledge into sunlight, but it wasn't the panorama that unfolded before her.

"Welcome to Ebal, Your Souci!" Jon swept his arm across the vista.

Susan stood silent, her face pale.

"Your Souci! What's the matter? Is it the height?"

"No, it's just that…I imagined a castle over there, and when I didn't see it, I felt, well…"

"Where did you imagine it?"

Susan pointed. Jon looked that way, squinting.

"What was it like, your castle?"

Susan described it in precise detail. The view from the mountain ledge was, except for the missing castle, exactly what Aunt Camellia had painted in the landscape that hung in Susan's living room.

"Camellia the Green lived in such a castle during her reign, Your Souci, and you can see its broken wall right there where you pointed if you look really hard."

Susan wished she hadn't said a thing. Unwilling to look at Jon just then, she stared into the sky. A moment later she saw a flash of gold, followed by a roar.

Gyldfen!

CHAPTER SIX

ROYAL FLIGHT

Susan clutched Jon. "How are we going to get away?"

"There, there, Your Souci," Jon soothed.

Susan raised wary eyes to the small gold flash in the sky, then looked at the path that wound down the side of the mountain, where she and Jon would be in plain view. With Susan clinging to him, Jon edged away from the lip of the ledge and back to the mountain wall. "I'm sure there's something in my bag we can use. Just you let go of me and I'll have a look." He slipped off his old leather bag and began to root in it.

"Something, something," he mumbled, pawing through the jumble, "where is the something to get us off this mountain?"

Susan wished she could see what he had in the bag. Her eyes darted back and forth from Jon, who was rummaging among who knew what, to the golden dot in the sky. "Do you have a magic rope?"

"Rope?" Jon raised his head from the bag. "Yes, I think so." He dove into his bag and surfaced with a small frayed coil.

"Is it magic?" she asked.

"It might be, Your Souci, but I don't know. Why do you want rope?"

"To rappel." Susan moved to the lip of the ledge and looked down. Thousands of feet to the ground. To rappel from the ledge to safety would require the most magic of ropes, and she had no confidence in the few sad loops Jon offered.

"What's 'rappel'?" Jon asked.

"It's…oh, never mind. It wouldn't work."

Another roar from Gyldfen sent Jon's hands groping in the bag again. "What's this?" he blurted.

"What, for goodness sake!"

Jon withdrew a blue lacquered stick. Susan snorted in frustration. "What's that going to do?"

Jon handled the stick a moment, admiring it. He raised it to his lips and blew a single sweet note into the air. Then he lowered the antique flute and returned it to his bag.

"Ever since I was given it, oh, ages ago, I'd always wondered what it would sound like, but I couldn't ever know, you see, because her majesty told me I must only blow it when— "

"When what? Why can't you just answer my questions?"

Jon raised his hand to hush her, listening for something. Susan frowned and clenched her teeth, but she listened too. No sooner did she discern the sound of beating wings than a thrashing cloud of blue feathers enveloped her. She lifted her hands to protect her face, holding them there even when silence descended a moment later.

"Your Souci?" Jon's question broke the quiet.

Susan lowered her hands and looked into the face of a large blue goose. A red ridge on the goose's dark beak rose to a spot between its eyes. A small tuft of red feathers crowned its head. Three other blue geese without red feathers on their heads crowded the ledge.

"You must be the new queen if the dragon's loose." The goose stared at Susan, who wondered that a goose could talk. But if a mailbox led to Ebal, she decided, why wouldn't geese talk there? "Not much to look at, are you, dear?" the goose continued. "I don't recall the Histories mentioning a grimy, sooty little majesty. I just hope none of the black comes off on my feathers."

The goose pointed her beak at Jon o'Gates. "Well, my fat little friend, it's high time we were off, what with a dragon hovering about. We four will be quite enough to carry you from that slug of a Gyldfen. I don't know how he keeps himself aloft on those pitiful bits of skin he calls wings."

Jon shouldered past one of the other geese, stood beside Susan and pulled off his hat.

"Your Souci, it is my very great pleasure to introduce Her Majesty Beatrice, Queen of the Blue Ebal Geese."

Queen Beatrice dipped her beak in acknowledgment.

"And," Jon added, "three of her finest courtiers."

The other geese bowed their necks.

"Your most exalted and speedy majesty," Jon went on, "let me present to you…ah, how should I put it?"

Queen Beatrice's beady eyes bored into him. He cleared his throat and rushed on. "Her Souci, Susan."

"Susan? Souci?" Beatrice aimed her pointed beak at Jon. "What is going on, my bumbling Keeper of the Gates? *Where* is Queen Camellia?"

"Well, you see, Your Majesty…"

"How dare you summon the ancient Escort of the Queen for a sooty child NOT named Camellia, a tangled-haired bit of grime with an alien title! And that cursed dragon loose! Just how do you come to be in the middle of this marsh muddle? And while you're at it, explain why in the name of the Giver we shouldn't feed you and this interloper to Gyldfen."

Jon stared at his scuffed brown boots. "It's…it's in the Histories, Your Majesty."

Beatrice stabbed her beak at Jon, stopping a hair's breadth from his nose.

Jon retreated a step. "The old, old part, Your Majesty. The very old part. It's all there. Really."

Beatrice glowered at him down the red ridge on her beak. Jon wrung his shapeless hat, twisting it in his hands. She glared a moment longer, then broke into laughter.

"What am I to do with you, my dear Jon o'Gates? I doubt you've read more than five pages of the Histories—and only the first ones with the big print and drawings. Imagine *you* telling *me* to read the Histories!"

The other three geese joined in their queen's laughter, and Susan smiled. She'd had a similar thought about Jon and his Histories not long before.

"I take it, then," added Beatrice, "that we're not going to Ingersoll and the coronation?"

Jon shook his head.

"Well, my little scholar, where?"

"I thought, Your Majesty, maybe you—with your agreement, of course Your Majesty—you and your courtiers might take us to Goose Bay near Ironwood."

Queen Beatrice narrowed her eyes. "You're going to Piotr's, aren't you? You want to check on what you never read in the Histories, don't you?" She stretched her neck forward and plucked at Jon's hair with her beak. "My dear fellow, best of Gate Keepers."

A great shadow fell on the crowded ledge, catapulting the geese into action. Two of them leapt into the air and hovered directly over Susan and Jon, loops of water weed dangling from their red webbed feet.

"Hands in wristlets!" ordered Beatrice.

Susan and Jon reached their hands through the loops of weed and held tightly as they were lifted a little ways into the air and maneuvered to a position a few inches above the backs of the other geese, Susan over Queen Beatrice's.

"Feet in scoops!" commanded Beatrice, lowering her neck so that a pouch opened on her back. Susan slipped her feet into it. When Beatrice raised her neck, the scoop closed firmly over Susan's feet.

Then they were airborne. Susan and Jon were supported by the geese above and below them. As they left the ledge on the mountainside, Susan looked down and felt her stomach drop. When she pulled on the wristlets, she got a quick honk of warning from the goose. Once her stomach rebounded and she got used to the sight of the ground far below, she relaxed, then jumped in fright at Gyldfen's roar, louder this time.

"Where is my slave queen?" he bellowed.

Susan yanked on the wristlets, provoking another honk. When she turned her head to look behind her,

Gyldfen was no longer a distant flash in the sky. He roared again, belching flame.

"That idiot," snorted Beatrice, "does he think he can spit fire as far as he can throw his voice?"

"But if he catches us…" Susan ventured.

"Catch us! Don't be absurd. The day old Golden Boy catches a Blue Ebal Goose is the day the sky falls. Hang on and watch this, my dear. Dive!"

Susan's head snapped back as the geese dropped into an eye-watering, breath-stealing dive. Her lungs burned from lack of oxygen, spots danced in front of her eyes, and she knew she was going to faint.

"Your Souci! Your Souci!"

Jon's voice. Susan raised her head. They were still flying, but slowly now. She could breathe. "I'm okay, Jon. I'm fine. Where are we?"

"Goose Bay, of course," replied Beatrice. "And nary a dragon in sight. Lumbering lout."

They spiraled down to a circular lake. The geese skimmed the lake's surface, lowered their webbed feet and skiied up onto the grassy shore. When Susan stood on the ground, she tilted her head back, scanning the sky.

"You won't find that slowpoke just yet, my dear." Queen Beatrice shook herself, realigning her back feathers. "You'll have time to get into Ironwood, I should think."

"Your most gracious and exalted majesty," Jon o'Gates began, "let me humbly express our highest humble—"

"Do stop being pompous, my dear fellow. It doesn't suit you at all. I gave you the ancient Summons of the Geese—you, not some stoop-shouldered, short-sighted, dance-hating reader of the Histories—for exactly this sort of occasion. I'm almost surprised you remembered you had, let alone found, it in that bag of jumble you tote. Thank the Giver she put the Summons in your hand when she did. You'd be dragon toast without it."

"Excuse me, Your Majesty," interrupted Susan, "but may I thank you for our rescue?"

"Of course you may, your...who are you, again? Your Souci? That can't be your title, surely. It sounds like one of our noodle-brained Gatekeeper's concoctions. But never mind now. Since you feel in my debt, I think

I'll ask for something in return."

Susan swallowed. What could she possibly do for the Queen of the Blue Ebal geese?

Beatrice grasped a few strands of Susan's grimy hair in her beak and held them a moment before dropping them in disgust. Then she plucked at Susan's filthy clothes. "First, clean yourself of this before you arrive at Ingersoll."

"But…"

Beatrice held up a wing. "Second, take care of Gyldfen once and for all."

Although Susan wanted to be clean and rid of the dragon, how could she do impossible things? Tears of hopelessness welled up in her eyes.

Beatrice lifted Susan's chin with the tip of her wing. "Many wish to be Queen, Your Souci, but few are." Beatrice contemplated her a moment before turning away and folding her wing. "Right now, however, I think you and Jon need to get to Ironwood before that gold piece of puffed pride comes pestering our part of the world. I look forward to when we meet again—and meet we shall, my little Souci, of that I'm sure. Then I'll be able to enjoy a proper dose of regal gossip."

Susan didn't feel certain of anything.

"Jon o'Gates," demanded Beatrice.

"Your Majesty?"

"Stop lollygagging and get Your Souci to Piotr's."

"Of course, Your Majesty! Right away. I don't know what I was thinking, Your Majesty." Tugging Susan by the arm, Jon quick-marched into Ironwood, his shoulder bag bouncing against one hip and Susan, who kept looking back at Queen Beatrice, bumping into the other.

CHAPTER SEVEN

PIOTR

They tramped for hours in Ironwood, the dim light filtering through slate-colored leaves. Susan felt closed in, not only by the forest but also by the difficulties every hour she spent in Ebal seemed to compound. And Aunt Camellia must be worried about her by now, perhaps fearful she'd drowned or been abducted, unless she *was* a witch or an ex-queen and had planned the whole thing, which would mean—what? She couldn't even guess.

She stopped walking. "I don't want to go to Piotr's," she said to Jon, "I want to go home." He didn't hear her. Whistling, happier in the woods than on the mountain, he walked on. Crossing her arms, Susan stood where she'd halted and spoke louder. "I'm not going any further." Jon continued along the path. "Didn't you hear me?" she shouted. "I said I'm not going any further. I want to go home."

Jon stopped in mid-stride and turned around.

"I don't want to be here. I don't belong here, and I'm nobody's queen."

"That's why we're going to Piotr's, Your Souci. He's the only one who knows enough about the Histories to tell us what to do."

"I don't need Piotr or your Histories to tell me it's all a mistake."

"Sometimes things only look like mistakes. If Queen Beatrice thinks you're the queen and going to see Piotr is a good idea..."

Susan uncrossed her arms and jammed her hands on her hips. Her chin jutted out. "I don't care what Beatrice said. I'm the one who's stuck in this mess, so I should know whether it's a mistake or not."

"Stop your racket," a gruff voice ordered. His eyebrows twitching indignantly, a scowling, red-bearded man stepped from behind a boulder. He was the same height as Jon but much older. The staff he held seemed more like a weapon than a walking aid.

"Piotr!" Jon cried.

Piotr turned his eyebrows on Jon, who fell back a

step. "Jon o'Gates. I might have known."

At that moment a blast of fire slammed into the crown of a nearby ironwood tree, pouring flames down the massive trunk. Susan shrieked and ran to Jon, who hid her behind the shelter of a boulder.

"Give me my slave queen!" boomed Gyldfen's branch-rattling voice.

Piotr's accusing eyebrows thrust themselves at Susan. "You're responsible for this!"

Another blast snapped off a large branch from the tree closest to Piotr, hurling it to the ground in sputtering flames.

"Enough!" Piotr shook his fist at the sky. He ran around the scorched branch and shoved Jon and Susan away from the boulder. "Get off my doorstep!"

He struck the rock with his staff, sparks erupting from the blow. The ground Susan and Jon had been standing on dropped away as a hidden door slid open. Piotr clattered down a set of stairs. When his head reached ground level, he paused and glowered at them. "Stay there, then, if you're so keen on annihilation." He disappeared from view.

Jon rushed Susan down the stairs as the door began to close. With a squeak of fright, he ducked his head before the sliding door hit it, lost his balance and tumbled down the remaining steps. The door closed, shutting out Gyldfen's attack and the light of day.

"Jon?" Susan asked in the dark. "Are you there? Are you okay?"

"All in one piece, Your Souci. What's a bit of a bounce if it gets you out of a dragon's way? Where's Piotr?"

"I don't know. When I got to the bottom, he was gone and then you fell down the stairs. I can't see a thing—where are the lights?"

"Here," Piotr answered brusquely. He was carry-ing a five-candle candelabra. Shadows leapt against the walls, revealing a small foyer. Next to a wall of coat hooks, a large stone vase bristled with walking sticks. Susan noticed Piotr's staff in the vase and his grey coat on one of the hooks. Four doors, one ajar, led from the entrance hall. Having set the candelabra in a sconce near the stairs, Piotr turned to Susan and Jon.

"You're both filthy; take a bath." He pointed to

one of the closed doors. "As Jon well knows, the tubs are in there. When you're done, you can find me here." He went through one of the other doors and shut it.

"What a rude man," Susan declared. "I thought you said he's your friend."

"He is, Your Souci. Well, actually, my father's friend, but he likes me too, in a distant sort of way. And he's not so bad, really, I mean, he knows so much about the Histories and he's…he did save us from Gyldfen."

"Hardly," Susan sniffed. "All he did was run into his house. Thanks to you, we followed him." She touched her hand to Jon's bearded cheek. "I'm sorry I yelled at you in the forest—I know it's not your fault."

Jon shrugged.

"Well, then," she said, "I suppose we'd better have our baths so that we can talk to Mr. High-and-Mighty about getting me home."

"If anybody can do it, Piotr can, Your Souci. But wait till you see the baths. Such warm water and fat towels!"

"Good. I'll be so glad to be clean again."

Through the door Piotr had indicated, they entered

a short hall. Susan noticed two more doors in front of her. A single large candle burned next to each door. "There's a bath in each room," Jon explained. "Why don't you go in the first one and I'll go in the next."

In her bathroom, which was bright with red candles, Susan found a large ceramic tub, a wooden chair, the fat towels Jon had praised, and an equally luxurious bathrobe. No mirror. No combs. No soap. And no apparent way to get water into the tub. She searched for buttons, knobs, recessed handles and little doors. "This is the stupidest bathroom I've ever seen," she declared, climbing into the tub to try a different point of view. All she saw was a long slit near the top of the tub at one end, which she assumed was to prevent the water from overflowing. No plug for the drain. "Great, just great. How am I supposed to take a bath? I bet this is Piotr's idea of a joke. Ha, ha."

She stormed out and, without knocking, flung open Jon's bathroom door. There sat Jon in the middle of the tub, soapsuds billowing around him. Instead of his shapeless hat, he wore a shapeless beret of lather.

"How'd you get water in that idiot tub?" she demanded. "And where'd you find the soap?"

"You, ah, sit in the tub, Your Souci, and the water comes in, you see, and when you stand up it drains away."

"Right. Sure it does. How silly of me not to think of that!" She pulled Jon's door shut as precipitously as she'd opened it, stormed back to her bathroom and got into the tub. "All right, fill!" She sat down. The slit she'd thought was an overflow drain immediately poured out a Niagara Falls of hot soapy water, filling the tub so quickly she had no time to take off her clothes.

The flow of water ceased when it reached her chest, soap bubbles foaming to her chin. Her clothes were soaked. "Terrific. Now I've got nothing dry to wear. Just one more thing." She smacked the water with her open hands. "I hate it here! I hate it!" She continued to strike the water, creating a tempest of soapsuds that left the survivors clinging to ceiling and walls.

Although she'd promised herself she wouldn't cry, tears seemed to come of their own accord. She removed her wet sneakers and peeled off her clothes, dropping each sodden piece over the side of the tub. Despite her vigorous scrubbing, the stubborn black from the Gold

Hall remained on her hands and hair. She assumed it was still on her face too. As her bottom lip began to tremble, she bit it and held it between her teeth till her tears dried up.

Jon knocked at her door. "Are you ready, Your Souci?"

"Just a moment." Susan stood up, and the water did what Jon said it would—drain. Minutes later she stepped out of the bathroom in a white bathrobe, her hair turbaned in a white towel.

"It didn't come off, did it?" she asked.

Jon shook his head. "Maybe Piotr'll have an idea."

"I'm not holding my breath."

The aroma of hot chocolate greeted them when they entered Piotr's cozy sitting room. Looking around, Susan saw an iron pot suspended over the fire in a miniature version of Aunt Camellia's baronial fireplace. Two empty mugs rested on the hearth, and overstuffed armchairs by the fireplace beckoned.

Piotr sat at a round table in the corner, poring over a large book with ancient covers. He had one hand on a page. The other hand pulled at one of his eyebrows.

Blue smoke curled from the carved pipe clamped in his mouth. Susan waited for him to look up from the book and notice them, but he didn't raise his eyes from the page he was reading. Annoyed, she said nothing, determined to out-wait him.

"Here we are, Piotr!" Jon called out.

Susan could have shaken him. She clenched her teeth when she saw Piotr give a smirk of victory. No, she decided, she did not like this man no matter what his good qualities might be. She wondered about Queen Beatrice's real opinion of him.

Piotr took the pipe from his mouth and looked at them, eyes shaded by his overhanging brows. "So I see. I trust your baths were satisfactory?" He put the pipe back in his mouth and returned his attention to the book.

"Oh, yes!" said Jon. "We feel much better, don't we, Your Souci?"

Susan had no intention of talking to Piotr if she could avoid it.

"Your 'Souci'?" He raised his head, eyebrows twitching as he scrutinized her.

Susan nodded curtly.

"The hot chocolate smells delicious!" Jon bubbled. "Those mugs are for us?"

Piotr noded and waved his hand at the mugs, inviting Jon to fill them.

Holding her mug of chocolate with both hands, Susan lowered herself into lotus position in front of the fire, her bathrobe spreading itself around her. Because her back was to Piotr, she missed his look of incredulity. Jon collapsed into the armchair closest to him, unconcerned when chocolate sloshed over the brim of his mug and onto his rumpled trousers.

Susan was delighted to discover that the hot chocolate never lost its marshmallow froth but remained thick and sweet all the way to the bottom. When she looked over at Jon to ask about seconds, she found he'd fallen asleep, his bearded chin resting on his chest.

"Since you two are done," intruded Piotr's rough voice, "there's some business to attend to before dinner."

Startled, Jon dropped his mug. It fell to the floor and broke, a brown puddle forming around the pieces.

"Oh dear," Jon mumbled. He looked over at Piotr.

"I'm sorry, I…it was an accident, you see, and, well, I'm…sorry."

"That's all right, Jon," Susan said. "It was Piotr's fault, so don't be upset." She twisted round to frown at Piotr, who was scowling at her. "What's this 'business'," she demanded in her best regal tone, "that it delays nourishment to hungry travelers?"

Piotr glowered, and his eyebrows sprang up like hackles. Susan maintained a steadfast silence. She had asked the question and was determined to have an answer. Piotr allowed the silence to lengthen, preserving his disconcerting glare as he puffed on his pipe. Jon fidgeted.

"Perhaps you're right," Piotr replied at last, his tone indicating the opposite. "Dinner first."

He clapped his hands twice. A moment later the door opened and a pair of short, round-faced, orange-furred creatures entered. They resembled small bears but with bigger, rounder ears, shorter snouts and long dark eyes that drooped at the corners. From the ear of one creature dangled a diamond earring. An emerald earring hung from the ear of the other, and a wide band of black fur circled their middles. They pushed an elegantly-set dining table that moved so quietly on its well-oiled wheels that Susan wondered if it floated. The white linen tablecloth billowed and the pink china, crystal glasses, and gold cutlery reflected the firelight.

"Bumbles," whispered Jon. "The diamond is Misha, the emerald Sharon."

The Bumbles efficiently transformed the sitting room into a dining area, pushing armchairs and Piotr's round table into corners and bringing chairs that matched the dining table. They guided Susan to the chair at the middle of the table so that she faced the fire. Piotr and Jon sat at opposite ends.

Before the Bumbles left the room, Misha filled the guests' glasses with a cobalt blue liquid.

"Blue Goose wine," Jon informed Susan, who decided it would be her favorite wine in memory of the flight on Beatrice's back. She raised the glass to her lips, but before she could taste the wine, Piotr called out, "A toast!"

Susan understood a toast was proper etiquette, but she suspected Piotr had proposed it just so she wouldn't be able to taste the wine in her own time. She pulled the glass away from her mouth and held it suspended, awaiting the toast.

"The Queen!" Piotr proposed.

Susan had read that, in Queen Elizabeth's time, Piotr's toast was the sort people used as a profession of loyalty. If Jon had offered the same toast, she would have drunk it. Piotr, however, was a different matter. She set her glass on the table and smiled at him. The bristling of his eyebrows and thrust of his chin told her she had guessed right: for whatever reason, he didn't want her to be the new queen, which meant the best way to irritate him was to pretend to be exactly that. By not drinking the toast, Susan knew she was implying that she was its object.

When Jon and Piotr had drunk the toast, Susan proposed another. "To Ebal!"

And of course Piotr could not refuse to drink to his homeland, as she had to the queen. The wine tasted all the sweeter for her double triumph over him.

The Bumbles re-entered, pushing serving tables loaded with covered dishes. As each dish was served,

Jon named it for Susan.

"Elmshorn with Ebal cheese sauce."

Not caring whether Piotr thought her ill-mannered, she ate a forkful—like asparagus.

"Roast Itzhoe." Lamb.

"Baked Doberan." Potato.

"Tollensee with Cammin." Delicious but not like anything she'd ever eaten.

"Bumbles are the finest cooks in all the world, Your Souci," Jon said.

She ate hungrily, enjoying the new tastes and flavors. Even if the food had been bitter, sour, and tart, she would have made a show of eating it because not eating when she was hungry signaled to others that she was upset. And though her stomach was tense from the antagonism between her and Piotr, she did not intend to let her host see that and scarcely looked his way throughout the meal.

"Piotr, you're hardly eating a thing," Jon commented. "You haven't even touched your Elmshorn, and I've never eaten better. I remember the last time I had Elmshorn was…no, that was the year I wandered—"

"Yes, yes," Piotr broke in. "That's quite enough. I have no wish to hear stories of your endless travels, time that should've been spent studying the Histories and inspecting the Gates, duties and responsibilities connected with the title you bear."

Susan noisily dropped her cutlery. How dare he rebuke Jon like that! Oh, for the chance to humiliate him and his ridiculous eyebrows. She snatched up her napkin, intending to throw it on her plate, when an idea occurred to her. She wiped her mouth with the napkin instead.

"Tell me, Piotr, why is the queen so important to Ebal?"

Putting his elbows on either side of his uneaten dinner, Piotr rested his bearded chin in his hands and looked at Susan as if she were a fool. "Because Ebal is a queendom."

"You mean kingdom," she corrected.

"I certainly do not! When I say something, I mean exactly what I say and nothing else. I believe I am possessed of the happy gift of clear speech, which conveys my meaning precisely."

"How fortunate for you. However, even when a queen rules a land, that land is still called a kingdom. You have only to look at Queen Elizabeth's long reign as a case in point. Although she was England's most successful monarch, she ruled a kingdom, not a queendom."

"Then she ruled over an illogical people in an illogical land," snapped Piotr, "because logic dictates that it should've been *called* a queendom to reflect the fact of the situation."

Susan saw the sense of Piotr's argument but refused to admit it to him, choosing to keep silent.

"Ebal," Piotr went on, "has always been a queendom, to which the Histories amply testify."

"But isn't there a missing section?" Jon asked. "At least, I think there is. I mean, I'm sure I heard something was missing from it or that it's incomplete somehow when I…That's it!—the same time I last had Elmshorn on Nine Beaches with—"

"Stop babbling, for goodness' sake, and make your point," Piotr demanded, turning his eyebrows on Jon.

Jon lost his nerve and said nothing more.

"His point," Susan intervened, "is that your conclusion is based on incomplete data and therefore no conclusion at all but an assumption only and subject to correction."

"Be that as it may…" said Piotr in a less aggressive tone.

"Don't the queens ever marry kings?" Susan asked, bored with the argument but curious about the way things seemed to be in Ebal.

"Never."

"Don't they want husbands and families?"

"The land is their husband and their subjects their children."

"Oh." Susan remembered that Queen Elizabeth had said something similar when she renounced any plan for a husband, cut off her hair, and dedicated herself to ruling England.

Susan pushed back her chair. Mentioning Queen Elizabeth had reminded her of Aunt Camellia and where she wanted to get back to. "Perhaps now is a good time for your 'business', Piotr."

"Aye, I think it is. Here, you Bumbles, clear all this away. I'll call for dessert—if there is to be dessert."

Piotr stood up and fished in his jacket pocket for his pipe. He jammed it in his mouth and took the few steps to where his table and Histories volume had previously rested. The Bumbles stopped clearing the dining table to replace Piotr's table and chair. From a drawer in his table Piotr took out a match and, striking it on the table's underside, lighted his pipe. With a practiced throw, he tossed the spent match into the fireplace and sat down. The noiseless Bumbles left the room with the dining and serving tables. Jon o'Gates sat in his armchair. And Susan, her face angled between the fire and Piotr, facing neither, able to see both, lowered herself into lotus.

"Go on," she said.

Exhaling smoke from his nostrils, Piotr tapped the tome in front of him. "This," he said,"provides three infallible signs that determine the validity of your claim to the queenship."

Until her arrival at Piotr's, Susan would've welcomed Piotr's 'proofs' to support her denial that she was the new Queen of Ebal. But now, she decided, she *would* be the queen, if for no other reason than to spite this arrogant bully. Let him name a hundred signs of proof—

she'd fulfill them all. In response to the challenge, she raised an eyebrow, indicating he was to name them.

Enraged, he bit so hard on his pipe stem that it snapped in half. The bowl dropped onto the Histories, spilling ash and burning tobacco. Sweeping the pipe to the floor in alarm, he blew the sparks and ash off the singed pages.

Jon leapt up to help but Susan put out her arm. "No!" she ordered. "Leave him to his broken pipe as he left you to your broken mug of chocolate."

Jon stood behind the barrier of her arm. "Yes, Your Souci."

Piotr glowered at her, the red hairs of his twitching eyebrows looking like tongues of flame. "First! Gyldfen is loosed."

"I did that. Surely you haven't forgotten my arrival on your doorstep."

"Second!—"

"And," Susan interrupted, "since Gyldfen considers me the queen, so should you."

"Second!" Piotr persisted. "You must bear two marks." Tracing the words with his finger, he read, "'The

Indelible Golden Grime and the Slash of Fire.'" He sat back, smiling victoriously.

Susan's desire to wipe the haughty grin from his face inspired her. She gave him a look of pity, savoring its effect as doubt replaced contemptuous certainty on his face. Then she stretched out her leg and flipped the bathrobe from it.

Piotr gaped at the long blistered wound stretching from her ankle to her knee, which she'd received from Gyldfen as she and Jon struggled to close the door after their escape from the Gold Hall.

"'The Slash of Fire'," she said simply, refolding her leg under the robe.

Next she held up her hands, the sleeves of the robe slipping down to her elbows and revealing the stark contrast between the clean skin of her arms and the unwashable black on her hands. She unwound the towel from her hair and shook it loose, its grimy state highlighted by the white robe. Finally, she raked her nails across the black stain on her forehead, scraping nothing away and leaving four welts on her skin.

"'Indelible Golden Grime', which your bath water

failed to remove—as well you know, since you saw me before and after I bathed."

Astonished, Piotr swallowed hard, then wet his lips.

"Third," he said in a hoarse whisper. "A member of an ancient Royal House of Ebal must give you the Task of Cleansing and the Task of Vanquishing."

The answer was so easy that Susan decided to lengthen the suspense. "Would you refill my mug, Jon?"

"Of course, Your Souci."

After she'd taken a sip of chocolate, set her mug down, and re-arranged the folds of her bathrobe, Susan addressed Piotr. "When Queen Beatrice answered Jon's call and flew us safely to Goose Bay—"

"What! Beatrice, Queen of the Blue Ebal Geese, *carried* you to Goose Bay? How...?"

"Jon blew the summons flute she'd given him."

Piotr looked at rumpled, clumsy Jon as if trying to see someone behind a disguise. "Queen Beatrice gave *Jon* such a thing?"

"Jon can tell you later—if you care to listen to the story of someone unread in the Histories and derelict in his duties to the Gates. I wish to finish my proof of queenship, if you don't mind."

"Yes, your maj—I mean, proceed," stumbled Piotr.

Susan smiled inwardly at Piotr's admission of defeat. Even before explaining that Beatrice had charged her with cleaning herself and destroying Gyldfen, she had won! Piotr believed she was the new queen. She had avenged her friend and subdued the pompous Piotr. How sweet the moment was. How superior she felt.

When she'd told how Beatrice had given her the two tasks, Piotr stood up. "Forgive me, Your Majesty." He bowed deeply and respectfully.

In that instant, Susan quailed, her sweet revenge suddenly bitter. Now that she'd proved she was the Queen of Ebal, how could she prove she wasn't?

CHAPTER EIGHT

HONEY CAKES

"I think now would be a good time for dessert," Piotr said.

He clapped his hands and, as if they'd been waiting outside the door, the Bumbles poked their round orange faces into the room.

"Honey cakes, my friends," Piotr said. "And a special treat as well. I believe something befitting the significance of the occasion is in order. You know what I mean." Instead of doing as he bid, Sharon and Misha remained where they were. "Oh, I almost forgot," he added. "Be good chaps and fetch the map."

Susan was puzzled. How could he call Misha and Sharon 'chaps' when anyone could see they were female?

The Bumbles still didn't go, but stood in the doorway, watching Piotr. He was patting his coat pockets. "And another thing. Bring me a pipe."

Sharon and Misha continued their vigil. Susan

smiled as she observed them—they obviously knew Piotr well.

"What are you ragamuffins loitering about for?" Piotr demanded. "Get!"

Although they did leave this time, they weren't long in returning. Misha, her diamond earring dancing, carried a pipe in one hand and tugged a large map on a wheeled stand. Sharon balanced a tray laden with fresh mugs of chocolate, a plate of pastries, and a mystery under an ornate silver cover, whose design Susan recognized— the crowd of figures she'd first seen on the gold shield in her aunt's hall.

Piotr took his pipe from Misha's hand, slipped it into his mouth and went to the volume of Histories on his table.

"You know, Piotr," Susan commented, "the Histories don't sound very historical to me—more like predictions and prophecies. Maybe they should be called Futures."

"I've always thought that too," Jon added.

"Have you now?" Piotr said. "For someone who's read so little of them, that's quite a statement to make.

Here, you Bumbles, set that down on the hearth, and put the map where we can see it."

While Misha maneuvered the map into place, Sharon put the tray on the hearth.

"Honey cakes, Your Souci!" Jon declared. "I could live on honey cakes!" Holding out a pastry to her, he gobbled one himself.

It looked like a swirl of honeycomb to Susan, but after the vocabulary lesson at dinner, she questioned Jon's use of words she knew. Could honey and cake in Ebal be what they were at home? One way to find out. She bit into the treat. "They *are* the same!"

Jon thought she meant something else. "Probably made from the same hive." He ran his tongue over his lips. "Malhotar. My favorite. Mind you, granicote honey is a close second, even though malhotars are prettier flowers—big and bright with hundreds of long, droopy petals, like a firework when it bursts." He reached for another honey cake, eating it in two bites. Pointing to the covered dish, he spoke with his mouth full. "What's under there?"

As Sharon lifted the lid to show him, Susan focused

on the cover itself, not what it hid. Like the view of Ebal from the mountain ledge, the shield design linked Aunt Camellia to Ebal. Did these connections mean her wild guess was true—that her aunt was a former Queen of Ebal?

"Coronation Creams!" Jon squealed. They resembled large cream puffs in the shape of crowns, studded with red and green Turkish delight jewels. Plucking one from the plate, Jon declared, "I can't remember the last time I…" His words disappeared into his bite of Coronation Cream. When he pulled the pastry away from his mouth, whipped cream smeared his beard.

"If I might have you over here a moment," Piotr requested, puffing on his pipe. With his middle finger, blackened from years of tamping burned tobacco, he pointed at the map. "The Queendom of Ebal."

Jon pushed his face close to the map, scrutinizing a faint red line. He twisted round, his finger on it. "Is this…? "

"You're getting it sticky!" Piotr bustled up and crowded Jon away. "Just look, don't touch. Now pay attention. This is Ironwood." He jabbed his middle fin-

ger at a spot near the bottom. His finger left a black smudge, which he immediately wiped away. "And this," he went on, careful not to touch the map with his finger, "is Gylden Mountain, in which lies the Gold Hall, Gyldfen's lair, already known to you."

Susan sat in Piotr's chair, focusing on the map and what Piotr had to say. The blue circle just to the right of his finger must be Goose Bay, she guessed.

"And these," Piotr said, his bony hand finger hovering over a cluster of inverted chevrons, "are the Rugged Mountains." His voice changed from a lecturing tone to one of fond remembrance, and Susan thought he looked longingly at the mountains. He cleared his throat, then stared at the floor for a moment. When he raised his head, Susan saw tears in his eyes. In his softened face, she glimpsed a younger, kinder man, and her heart lost much of its hardness towards him.

"You were there once?" she asked.

He nodded. "With her majesty, Camellia the Green."

An image of her aunt twisting her emerald ring flashed in Susan's mind.

"You journeyed with the Queen to the Old One?" Jon breathed.

Piotr nodded again.

"Then the red line is…"

"The Narrow Path to the Star Flower," finished Piotr. "Yes, my dear friend's son, this is the Queen's Map. Your time has come to travel it."

"But… "

"No, the task is yours." He nudged Jon back to his spot in front of the map. "Study it well. The Queendom depends on your skills now, much as I have too often said otherwise." Piotr draped his arm over Jon's shoulder as the two looked at the map, one remembering, the other imagining what would be.

Witnessing such a moment was worth any number of dragons chasing her, Susan thought, feeling tears of her own spill.

When Piotr and Jon at last moved away from the map, Jon glanced at Piotr, expecting him to say something. Piotr stayed resolutely silent. Finally understanding, Jon straightened his round shoulders, took a deep breath and spoke to Susan.

"We are to journey the Narrow Path to the Rugged Mountains, Your Souci," he began in his best formal manner, "because you must consult with the Old One." Unable to contain himself any longer, he rushed on: "And I'm to guide you there, the whole way where I've never been before and always wanted to go but never dared to hope I ever would since I could never find the map that showed the road I could only go on if the queen appeared and I was chosen because of the ancient law forbidding wanderers like me to trespass but here you are and we're not wanderers because we're the ones! We're going on the Narrow Path!"

Susan stood up and presented her best smile. "When do we leave?"

"As soon as you're outfitted," Piotr answered.

He went to the door and opened it. "Bumbles," he called out. "Ready two travelers for the Rugged Mountains!" He looked back at Jon and Susan. "I think I'll just give the dear chaps a hand. You can meet me by the stairs in a few minutes."

Jon bounced over to Susan. "Isn't it wonderful!" Then his eyes went round with surprise. He brought his face close to Susan's and touched her cheek with his fingers.

"What?" she asked.

"The Grime. Some of it's gone!"

Susan recalled her tears and wondered.

CHAPTER NINE

THE GATES OF CHOICE

Susan and Jon stepped into the foyer. Jon's jacket hung from the row of pegs and his battered brown boots slouched on the floor below it. The stairs invited them up to their journey. As Piotr's voice rumbled from behind one of the four doors, Susan pictured the Bumbles' eyes, horizontal and happy that Piotr had changed from a gruff and overbearing man to the kind person he'd once been. Susan hoped it wasn't temporary. Misha and Sharon deserved this better fellow.

"Please let it be true," she whispered.

"What was that, Your Souci?"

"Nothing, Jon. Just thinking out loud."

"You do that too? I've always figured thinking out loud is a walker's hazard—no, hazard's not right—problem maybe—no, that's not it either. It's more like the callus a woodcutter gets on his hand. When you're alone and wandering and there's so much to remark on, well, you just remark, don't you? And after a while you can't tell whether you're talking inside your head or into the air, not that it really matters anyway, except when you visit somebody's house."

Jon eyed the walking sticks. "You know, my hand feels more comfortable when it can hold a good stick on a long ramble."

He stepped over to the vase and surveyed the sticks, putting his hand on a knobby brown one. With a glance over his shoulder to make sure Piotr wasn't coming, he pulled it out. "Perfect. Just the one for me."

"I see you've anticipated my parting gift," Piotr said as he entered the foyer, a bundle of clothes in his arms.

"You mean I can really have it? I'll never lose it, Piotr, I promise. It's so beautiful! I think I've wanted it forever, from the first time my father brought me here and I saw it and he told me not to touch anything but I just had to, you see, because it was calling me and now to think it's actually mine! You're sure I can have it?"

"Yes, lad, I'm sure. I suspect it's been a tad lonely all these years waiting for you."

Jon held it out to Susan. "Just feel it, Your Souci,

and tell me it isn't the most perfect stick ever!"

Susan took it and ran her hand down its curved and polished length, tracing the knobs. "It's a lovely stick, exactly the right one for you."

"Perhaps her majesty would like one," suggested Piotr.

"Of course!" Jon declared, taking Susan's hand and dragging her to the vase. Go on, Your Souci, pick one."

"Please, Your Majesty," Piotr encouraged.

Susan stared at the jumble of sticks crossing one another and jutting out at odd angles from the vase. She spotted a dark one that looked free from the crowding interference of the others and slipped it out.

"It's very straight," she commented, sliding her hand down its length. Black with slashes of red. Not a curve, knob or knot of blemish on it. She planted the stick on the floor, holding it with one hand. "And it certainly feels good."

She looked over to her friends. Sharon and Misha had appeared while she'd been making her choice. All four applauded.

"What?"

"You've chosen the Red Thorn," Piotr said.

"So?" Then she rolled her eyes. "I get it—another test."

"Only the true queen can choose the true stick," Jon blurted.

"By which he means," Piotr explained, "the one that's straight and flawless." His eyebrows raised themselves at Jon. "I thought you didn't read the Histories."

Jon shuffled his feet. "I...uh...sometimes glanced at the odd page."

"'Sometimes' indeed," Piotr growled. "Well, Bumbles, we'll take the Red Thorn as confirmation of red as her majesty's color, then. Right?"

Sharon's and Misha's nodding sent their earrings sparkling. Piotr held out the clothes to the Bumbles. When they approached Susan, she shrank back, clutching her robe.

"I can't dress in front of you—I'm not wearing anything!"

"Ah, yes," Piotr mumbled. "There is that."

Sharon and Misha patted Susan's arms and signaled her to go into the sitting room. Some minutes later, she emerged with both Bumbles, who immediately left the foyer.

The short baggy coat and baggy trousers Susan wore were identical to Jon's, except that hers were red instead of green. Her brown boots resembled Jon's too. In addition, she sported a red traveling cape with a brimmed hood. She decided the cape was better than the hooded ponchos she wore on outdoor expeditions. Not only could it be left open, it was easier to slip on and off.

"I feel like Little Red Riding Hood," she said, spreading the sides of her cape.

Jon looked up from his boot-pulling-on crouch. "She went to the Rugged Mountains too?"

"Never mind."

"You look fit to travel to the Old One now, Your Majesty," Piotr said.

"Just why do I need to go to the Old One anyway?"

"Two reasons," Piotr replied. "First, to learn how to cleanse yourself of the Golden Grime. And second, to learn how to destroy Gyldfen. Then you can be crowned at Ingersoll."

Susan puckered her brow. She suspected that her

119

tears had something to do with cleaning the Grime. But if tears themselves were the cleanser, she reasoned, then her face should be pristine by now—what she'd cried in the Golden Hall alone was enough to drown a dragon. And since they hadn't cleaned her at all, but seemed to have made her dirtier, then it must be the kind of tears that were important. But what kind were those?

At the moment, though, that didn't matter. What did matter was that, if she were right about her tears, then the Old One had nothing to do with The Cleansing. It also meant the Old One probably had nothing to do with the death of the dragon either, because destroying the dragon was a bigger version of cleaning dragon dirt. Susan silently thanked Papa for the time he'd taken to teach her how to reason clearly, even if she hadn't appreciated his insistence on it.

She smiled at Piotr's craftiness. He'd given reasons for her journey to the Old One that would be accepted by someone who didn't know tears were the cleanser of Golden Grime and couldn't reason. Too bad for Piotr.

"What's the real reason?" she asked.

"The 'real reason'?" Piotr broke into a sudden fit of coughing. "What do you mean?"

"What do you mean, 'What do I mean?'" countered Susan, banging her stick on the floor. Her performance amazed her. It was like watching a movie.

"I mean...that is to say, I..." Piotr stopped stammering and bowed. "Forgive me, Your Majesty."

"I'm sure he didn't mean what he...what he meant, Your Souci, or what he, uh, thought he meant to mean," Jon added.

"Your Majesty is quite right," conceded Piotr at last. "I mistakenly gave the *outcomes* of her journey to the Old One as the *reasons* for undertaking it. Let not her majesty look too harshly on an old man's failing mind, I pray."

Lying dog, Susan thought. *Your mind is failing as badly as Jon's heart is losing its wanderlust.*

"Well?" Susan brought her walking stick to a spot directly before her and placed both hands on top. Resting her chin on her hands, she stared at Piotr.

The Bumbles reappeared. They looked at Susan, then Piotr. Then they dropped into their own short-legged variation of Susan's lotus and waited.

"Would Your Majesty allow Jon to fetch my chair?" Piotr asked. "My bones..." He did look tired. Even his eyebrows drooped.

Susan raised her chin a hair's breadth, giving a tiny nod. She didn't break eye contact with Piotr.

Jon scuttled into the sitting room and, with much bumping and muttering, got the chair out of the room and behind Piotr. When Piotr was settled, Jon stood behind him.

Susan raised an eyebrow at Piotr like a conductor raising her baton to an orchestra. Time to begin.

Piotr cleared his throat. "It has been some little while, Your Majesty, since this queendom has had a monarch. Since Camellia the Green, in fact. Now *there* was a queen. In my heart I have long hoped to see another great queen. And I still hope."

If she hadn't been so determined to leave Ebal, Susan thought she would show him she could be just such a queen.

"Between the time of her departure and your arrival," he went on, "Ebal—and I, in particular—have been plagued by pretenders to the throne. I say 'I' because the unscrupulous masters of those brainless things brought them to me to validate. Fools!"

Piotr's bristling eyebrows needed a moment to calm down. "As a result—and my everlasting shame has been to only realize it this day—I have become a bitter, old man in my service to the queendom. When I look at my long-suffering Bumbles and the son of my dearest friend afraid of me—of *me*!—well, it gives me pause, Your Majesty, it gives me pause."

Jon put his hand on Piotr's shoulder. "I wasn't really afraid, you know. It was just that you were always reading the Histories, you see, and snapping at me whenever I came to invite you for a ramble because Father said you were a great rambler and I could learn so much from you but you never would—ramble, I mean—and so I don't quite know what I didn't learn from you not coming with me except that it's nicer to explore with somebody than nobody, especially with somebody like you who's been all the way to the Rugged Mountains and I'm not even sure where I find the Narrow Road to guide Her Souci on."

Piotr patted Jon's hand. "Don't worry, lad, I'll show you. It's not far from here."

"It isn't? What does it look like, when can we see it, can we go now, won't you come a little way with us, what about the Bumbles, does it really go through the Malabar Swamp?"

Susan banged her stick on the floor. "Jon o'Gates!"

Jon tried to curb his eagerness, looking as apologetic as he could. "Sorry, Your Souci."

"Thank you."

Piotr patted Jon's hand again. "It's all right, lad. It won't be long now." He turned his attention to Susan. "You must travel the Narrow Road to make your free choice before the Old One, the only one with the keys to open the Gates of Choice: the Queen's Gate, if you choose to rule the queendom; or the Gate of Going, if you choose to return."

For Susan, the choice was an unimagined possibility. For the others, her possible choice was unimaginable.

CHAPTER TEN

THE NARROW PATH TO THE STAR FLOWER

Stay or go?

Now that she had the chance to leave Ebal, Susan wasn't sure she wanted to. The energy she'd spent convincing Piotr that she was the new queen had almost convinced her too. She'd only done it, she said to herself, because Piotr had been so mean and needed to be taught a lesson. But look at the result.

If she stayed, she'd be a hypocrite in Jon's eyes. How could he forget her angry protests that she wasn't the queen and that it was all a horrible mistake, not to mention her whining to be sent back to her aunt's? Mind you, who could blame her? How many people had to endure a stupid mailbox that turned into a tunnel leading to a golden cavern with nobody to explain anything to her? And when there finally *was* somebody, it turned out to be a dragon who wanted to enslave her for goodness knew what. No, she decided, her behavior on that score was justified. It wasn't her fault. Confusion just did not bring out the best in her, that was all.

If she left Ebal, she'd be welching on the debt she owed Queen Beatrice for her rescue. She'd be a coward for running away from the tasks Beatrice had assigned her. She knew her tears held the key to cleaning the Grime. Remaining a coward in her own mind was intolerable. Even taking care of Gyldfen might be possible, she reasoned. Besides, she did want to see Beatrice again and have that chat the blue goose had promised.

Then there were the Bumbles. They'd shown her such loving attention and dressed her in the special clothes they'd made—wait till Jon saw what her cape transformed into. Could she be ungrateful to them?

Stay or go? She needed to know something first. "Piotr."

"Majesty?"

"Why do I have to go to the Old One to choose? Why can't I do it here? And please don't tell me the Histories say I have to, Keeper of the Books."

"How did you know my true title?"

"Not again," Susan muttered. Why had she added

the phrase that popped into her head? "I heard Jon mention it," she lied.

"Impossible!"

She decided to brave it out. "Nothing could be more possible. He's wandered around talking to everybody in Ebal. How do you know he didn't meet some long-forgotten Keeper of the Books who'd been banished to an unvisited corner of the land where he'd spent his thousand years of exile reading a moldy copy of the Histories?"

Piotr whirled on Jon, his eyebrows so far out they threatened to clutch the shocked Keeper of the Gates. "You spoke to Bildad!"

"Never mind Bildad!" Susan interjected. "Why do I have to go to the Old One? Bildad can wait—the future of Ebal can't!" She hoped her appeal to Ebal would get Piotr's attention back. When would she learn to shut up?

Her words set off a terrible struggle in Piotr. His hands clutched the arms of his chair like talons. He clenched his jaw till the cords in his neck stood out and his face turned red. The chair shook as he battled for control of himself.

Susan cast a worried look at Jon. "What's the matter with him?"

"I don't know, Your Souci. I've never seen him like this." He put both his hands on the old man's shoulders. "May the Giver help him."

Minutes passed before Piotr relaxed his grip on the chair and unclenched his jaw. He was pale with exhaustion.

"Piotr?" Susan inquired. "Are you okay?"

Several seconds passed before he nodded. At last he spoke. "You correctly remind me of my duty, Your Majesty. It seems so long since her former majesty…" His voice trailed off.

"Piotr?" Susan prompted.

"I've unwisely cloistered myself here with little to do but wait and hope. Instead of following my good friend's advice to ramble with him in the bright light of day, I fear I've confused too many events from too many ages. I scarcely know the past from the present or the future from the past."

"There, there," Jon soothed. "Someone had to confuse them."

There was a moment's silence as Piotr and Susan tried to puzzle out what Jon meant. Then Piotr laughed and life flowed into his face. He straightened in the chair and addressed Susan. "The answer to your question, Your Majesty, is…" He closed his eyes and recited the words from memory. *"Solvitur ambulando."*

"That's Latin!" Susan said, astonished, feeling the tingling sensation she'd first noticed when she sat on her Persian carpet and which had recurred a number of times recently.

"I always wondered what tongue it was," he added. "Her Majesty never said, only bidding me remember it. What does it mean?"

It means, Susan thought to herself, Aunt Camellia had me take Latin lessons to translate this. And since I can, I suppose I should. "It could stand for, 'He/she/it is released by walking' or 'It's solved in walking' or some combination of the two. Whatever fits."

"Perhaps Her Majesty intended it for both of us," Piotr suggested after a moment's reflection.

"What do you mean?" Susan wasn't sure she wanted

to know.

"'It's solved in walking' applies to you because you must walk to the end of the Path to make your choice. 'He's released by walking' applies to me because I'll be released from the Histories by wandering Ebal like Jon."

"You can start now," Jon declared. "You said you'd show me the Narrow Path and once you have, you can ramble till we get back from the Rugged Mountains. Get your boots and stick, Piotr. There's so much to see!"

"Right you are, lad." Piotr slapped his thighs. He stood up and turned to his coat on the wall peg.

In their hurry to get ready, they momentarily forgot Misha and Sharon. But as Jon set his boot on the first step leading up to the forest floor, the Bumbles appeared beside Susan with one more item for her journey.

"Your own treasure bag!" Jon exclaimed.

Susan slipped it over her shoulder. "Thank you Misha, thank you Sharon. It's beautiful." She began to cry. "You've been so kind, so…Bumbly." She gave up trying to speak and fell into their furry arms, crying for love of such good creatures. When they wiped her tears away, she didn't notice the black drops of Golden Grime on their orange paws.

After one last quick embrace, Susan hustled after Piotr and Jon, who had already gone up the stairs. Once outside, she took the middle position between the two little men. Piotr set a quick pace and Jon chattered away while Susan walked in the silence of her own thoughts. Hours later, they reached the edge of Ironwood. They gazed on the charred remains of what was once a meadow.

"Typical dragon pique," Piotr remarked.

"What do you mean?" Susan asked.

"When Gyldfen failed to catch you and Jon, and failed to do any damage to Ironwood, he came here and torched the meadow. I'll be glad when you've made an end to him once and for all, Your Majesty."

Right, thought Susan.

"Mind, there is some good for us out of all this," Piotr added.

"What?" Jon asked.

Piotr took a few paces into the burned-up field and began scuffing at the ground with the toe of his boot.

Jon came up beside him. "What are you doing?"

"Looking."

Piotr continued his scuffing, occasionally looking back to Ironwood as if getting his bearings, then shifting his position accordingly.

Jon scuffed too. "What are we looking for?"

"This!" Piotr pointed with the toe of his boot.

Susan and Jon peered at the ground. "What?" Susan asked.

"The marker for the Narrow Path to the Star Flower," Piotr said.

Engraved on a stone marker level with the ground was a simple design.

"The triangle on the bottom represents the Rugged Mountains," he explained. "The line with the point is the direction, and the six-pointed cross is the star of Gilead, which hovers over the Path. The markers will guide you on the Path."

"Why do we need markers?" Susan asked. "Why can't we just sight ourselves with the star?"

"Because the Path isn't straight, Your Majesty. At every turning you'll find a marker—likely overgrown or covered with debris—that points the Path's direction. If you were to choose your own direction you might sometimes guess right, but most often you'd be wrong. And way leads on to way and soon you'd be lost. Though you might find your destination in the end, you'd arrive late and full of regret. You must trust to the Path's turns, not yours."

Piotr knelt down by the marker and, tracing the engraved design with his finger, he recited:

> *"When atop the thirteenth flight of stairs*
> *And at the golden needle stand…"*

"I know that!" Jon interrupted, joining Piotr in the last lines:

> *"Then from the plume of white feather hair*
> *Shall arise the great Gilead."*

"I hate riddles," Susan grumped. "People always use them when they can't or won't answer a question. I think it's cheating."

"But they sound so nice," Jon said. "And you can spend forever imagining answers—it's like a ramble in your mind."

"Touch the marker, Your Majesty," Piotr said.

Susan bent down and stretched her fingers over the design but didn't touch it. She drew her hand back and looked at Piotr.

"You felt it without touching," he said.

"What is it?" she whispered.

Jon knelt down and traced the design with his finger. "It tingles! Just like when I put the key into the Gate."

"The Namsat," Piotr said.

"But what is it?" Susan entreated.

"The Namsat is the spirit of Ebal or maybe its energy. It's difficult to explain. The Histories say almost nothing about it, as well I know. What little I've learned, I've gleaned from myth and from what Camellia the Green told me. Besides the female members of the royal houses, the Keepers occasionally feel the Namsat, mostly when they're directly involved in their royal duties, like now and when Jon inserted the key in the right Gate." He picked up a handful of charred grass and rubbed it into ash. "But only the Camellias…"

"What?" Susan prodded.

"Only they have the power…"

Susan suddenly understood why there were never kings of Ebal. "To use the Namsat," she finished.

Piotr nodded. "Her Majesty said it was more like following it. That's why the Camellias are important. Without them to guide us, the queendom wanders off course and troubles abound, as eventually happens when we rule ourselves between their reigns. Why we can't seem to manage without a Camellia has something to do with not being attuned to the Namsat, but what that is or why remains a mystery. Should Your Majesty stay and rule Ebal, it is my hope to live long enough to learn the what and why of the Namsat for Ebal's future well-being."

"That's very noble of you, Piotr," Susan said. "With so little in the Histories, where will you look?"

"Jon has shown me the way, though I've long resisted following it."

"I have?" Jon asked, astonished.

"Yes, my lad—in the amazing amount of information you've accumulated from your rambling—the wisdom in your fund of stories and something I sense that links those treasures you tote about. I'm convinced the answer lies in Ebal itself, and the only way to find out is to wander it as you have. That and listening to your tales and examining your treasures, all of which I look forward to doing on your return from the Rugged Mountains."

"Piotr…" Jon began, but was so overcome he didn't quite know how to go on.

"Well, I must say, it's a pleasure to hear you tongue-tied for once." Piotr smiled. "I never thought I'd see the day, or that I should be the cause of it."

Susan added her smile to Piotr's as Jon stared at his foot scuffing the ground. The a thought occurred to her: "Is the Namsat why Gyldfen is chasing me? Could he control the Namsat through me?"

Piotr shrugged. "Bend it, perhaps, or pervert it through you. Mercifully, it's never happened, but it is a danger."

"And there are other threats?"

"Besides Gyldfen? Yes, Your Majesty. Bildad, for instance."

"What about him?"

"He was a Keeper whose knowledge of the Namsat

136

led him to lust for its power. He aspired to be the first King of Ebal. He corrupted his own spirit and turned himself into a monster."

Susan didn't think she wanted to know any more. "I see." She turned from Piotr and headed back to Ironwood, her head lowered, eyes on the ground.

"Your Souci!" Jon called, starting after her.

Piotr stopped him. "Let her be, Jon. We'll sit here and you can tell me about your rambles."

Susan returned an hour later, giving neither apology nor explanation. "This is as far as you come with us, isn't it?" she said to Piotr.

"Yes, Your Majesty. Stay true to the path and you'll find the answer you seek. Stay true to Jon and he'll take you to the doorstep of your quest. There's no one better."

He knelt and kissed her hand. She shivered at the touch of his eyebrows brushing her wrist. "If we meet again, Your Majesty, it will be at Ingersoll."

Then he embraced Jon. "Enjoy the journey, lad. There's none other like it."

Jon had trouble finding his voice as tears glistened

on his cheeks. Susan's face was wet from crying.

Piotr wore a smile. "I think I'll just wander down to Goose Bay and tweak the tail feathers of that reprobate blue queen. *Solvitur ambulando,* Your Majesty – the answer's in the walking."

He waved and walked back into Ironwood, leaving Susan and Jon alone in the blackened remains of the meadow feeling the weight of parting from a good man.

"*Solvitur ambulando*," Susan choked out at last. "Be released in walking."

Jon wiped his tears with the sleeve of his coat and adjusted his leather bag. "Ready, Your Souci?"

Susan opened her Bumble bag in search of a tissue, found a handkerchief and dabbed her tears with it. She smiled at Jon. "Ready."

Jon stared at her. "Your Souci! The Grime—more is gone!"

She looked into the handkerchief and saw black drops lying there. She thought she understood the mystery of her tears now.

"I know. Let's walk, Jon."

CHAPTER ELEVEN

THROUGH THE GLOOM

A few steps after they'd started, Jon stopped and shook his head, clucking to himself.

"I'm sorry, Your Souci. Here's Piotr showing me the marker with the right direction and saying I was a good guide, and do I take a bearing to keep us in the right direction? Of course not—I just set off as if I'm on another ramble to see what there is to see instead of a special journey. But since we've barely begun and it's not too late to make amends, as my mother used to say, let's do the right thing and go back to the marker. I'll dig out the Saluki compass—a real treasure, Your Souci—wait till you see it! Such navigators, the Salukis. They gave it to me as a memorial of the opening of the Queen's Lighthouse, which they began in the reign of Camellia the Green, you know, and dedicated the very day I wandered into their port, which I went to because I'd heard so much about their incredible ships—'as swift as thought,' the poet Remoh wrote—and I had a hankering to see those ships for myself. They're famous—maybe you've heard of them?—they have no tiller because all the navigator has to do is *think* where he wants to go and the ship obeys. Isn't that marvelous?"

"Thinking ourselves to the Old One would be my idea of marvelous."

Jon looked up from pawing the jumble of treasures in his bag. "Don't wish that, Your Souci! We'd miss the whole trip then, and I'm sure there's so much to see on the Path. Just think of it—the Narrow Path! Hardly anyone travels it—only once in a queen's reign and sometimes not even then—it's more famous than even Saluki ships–it's the Real Thing, it's… But, to cut matters short, as Piotr would say, and get to the point. When I introduced myself—to the Salukis, I mean—what do I find but that they'd heard of me. Imagine, me known to Saluki navigators! Well,"—Jon bent to the search of his bag again—"we talked about this and that, as travelers do, and then they—ah, here it is—they gave me this fabulous instrument." He held it up, gleaming in the sunlight. "I've hardly used it, since I tend to wander around without much need for compass directions because when you're rambling it doesn't matter where you go, does it? But treasures are treasures and you never know when you might need one, so it's good to have a bag to keep them in because you can always find something to eat or somewhere to sleep, but you can't always find treasures because treasures are a different matter altogether—you never know when you'll discover their worth. That's what makes them treasures, you see, and that's why I always carry mine." He patted his old leather bag. "Take the goose whistle. Who would've thought such a delicate thing would save us from Gyldfen? So, what do you think of the Saluki compass?"

Susan was familiar with navigational aids, thanks to her historian papa and the wilderness camp training Aunt Camellia had sent her on. The compass Jon held did not appear as special as he claimed. "It's lovely."

"Wait till you see inside." He flipped up the cover and handed the compass to her.

She was prepared to admire it in a polite, non-committal way, not anticipating much beyond the ordinary. After all, what could one expect of a compass, Saluki or otherwise? One look at the design on the gold cover told her how mistaken she was.

"That design…" She stared at the finely engraved pattern. "It's..." She thrust the compass into his hand and reached into her bag for the handkerchief she'd wiped her tears with moments ago.

"Look, Jon," she said, spreading it open.

"They're the same! I wish Piotr were here. Maybe the Histories have something to say about this."

"Maybe." The pattern on the Persian rug again. When she'd looked into the handkerchief the first time, the pattern hadn't registered—the spots of Grime cleaned by her tears had been all she could take in. A new thought occurred to her. In trying to make her life go the way she wanted, she'd made herself angry and miserable. Was it possible that true control lay in following something like the Namsat?

While Susan was considering this idea, Jon concerned himself with the business at hand. He knelt down to the marker to take his bearing.

"Your Souci! The needle."

"What needle?"

Jon held up the compass. She glanced at a typical floating compass needle, more ornate than most, but a compass needle nonetheless. Then she looked at the direction arrow on the marker. "They're identical too."

"Yes, they're...no, look. The Saluki needle ends in a flower with one, two, three...six petals, not a star. And see, because the flower is hollow, the bearing is inside it so you can't get the direction wrong. Isn't that clever?"

She held her handkerchief close to Jon's face. "What do you see in the center of this design?"

Jon scrutinized the pattern. "It's the flower. Not only that, look. If you join these two broken lines running to the edge of the circles—" he touched them with his fingers— "then you have the compass needle."

"What's in the middle of the pattern on the compass cover?"

Jon squinted at it. "A star."

"There's something in the center of this one too, but I can't make it out. Looks like a fat squiggle."

"Maybe some of the Golden Grime smudged it. I think all this is a sign we're doing what we're supposed to be doing, Your Souci. Here we are on the Narrow

143

Path to the Flower Star and what do we find?" He held up his hand and listed his points on his fingers. "First, a Saluki compass needle like the Path marker. Second, a design on the cover like the design in your handkerchief. Third, a flower-star at the center of both patterns." He looked at his three fingers. "Treasures have a way of talking to you, I find."

Susan folded the handkerchief and put it back in her bag. "Take your bearing, Jon, and let's go."

"It looks like we head towards that wood in the distance. We'll probably find another marker there to tell us where we go next."

"Right."

They adjusted their bags and marched side by side through the dragon-devastated meadow, sticks in hand.

"What if Gyldfen sees us in the open?" Susan asked near the middle of the field.

Jon quickened the pace. By the time they reached the wood, they were running. Such was the momentum of their fear that they entered the shelter of the trees before stopping to look for a marker. Safe from spying eyes, they fell panting to the ground.

"If we race along like this, Your Souci, we'll be there in no time."

"I'm sorry, but my fear...it wasn't very queenly."

"Don't you worry, Your Souci. Fear's...well, what I mean is, there's fear and then there's fear, if you get my drift. Fear that stops you doing something worthwhile isn't good, of course, but fear that stops you doing something careless is good. It's telling the difference that's the thing. Take my ramble to the Pugdun Gorge. I'd climbed out to—"

Susan pointed and screamed. Gyldfen was gliding towards their forest shelter with such speed that he blurred into a kaleidoscope of golden scales and scarlet claws. Jon grabbed Susan and clamped his hand over her mouth. "Don't scream, Your Souci!" His mouth pressed on her ear. "I don't think he's seen us—he'd be spewing fire if he had."

She struggled against Jon's arms, wanting to run away. Watching the dragon approach was like being back in Gyldfen's cavern, rooted to the golden floor by his mesmerizing eyes, powerless to flee. Every fear she'd ever felt coalesced into a single gold shadow swallowing everything but itself. Gyldfen seemed determined to crash into the very trees they cowered under and gobble up their branch-pinioned bodies. Susan stopped squirming, terrified rigid in Jon's arms. Just before she thought the monstrous jaws would crush her and the horrid tongue snake around her bleeding body, the backdraft from Gyldfen's last-minute ascent blew branches off the trees and tumbled her and Jon further into the forest.

"Your Souci." Jon shook Susan's shoulder.

She lay face-down on the ground. When she rolled over, her face was a smear of tear and dirt stains, her grime-encrusted hair a nest of leaf bits and broken twigs. "Oh, Jon!" She flung herself into his arms, sobbing with relief and gratitude. She pushed herself away at last, wiping her face with her sleeve. "I must look terrible."

"Well, just a little. I think I'll take a peek, Your Souci, to make sure Gyldfen's really gone. I'm pretty sure he is, but it's best to be sure before barging into the open."

She clutched his hand. "Don't go."

He patted her hand. "Don't worry, Your Souci. I'll stay under the trees." He tugged his hand until she let it

146

go.

"Take care, Jon. Please."

"Of course. A man can't be too cautious with a dragon around."

Susan distracted herself with pulling twigs out of her hair and then searching in her bag to see what 'treasures' it might contain. She was munching a honey cake when Jon returned with a puzzled expression on his face.

"What's wrong?"

"No, no, he's gone, Your Souci. And I found the marker, but it's funny-looking."

She offered him a piece of honey cake. "What is?"

"Ah, nothing like honey cake to restore a wanderer. But the marker. Come see."

Susan shook her head.

"Oh. Well, the needle's zigzagged. Like this." He drew a zigzag pointer on the forest floor. "Strange, eh?"

"Maybe it means our route through this forest is a zigzag. How many were there?"

"How many what?"

"Zigs and zags."

"You think the number of them on the needle will

be the same number as on the Narrow Path? I'll go check."

"Eleven," he said when he returned.

Susan stood up and adjusted her bag, ready to start. "Good. Let's go."

Jon led the way, counting out each sharp turn they made. "Zag one. Zig two. Zag three…"

Because Jon was quiet, absorbed in keeping to the path in the deepening gloom of the forest and not talking, Susan dropped her head and let her mind wander where it would—into her Bumble bag and one particular treasure, over the curious coincidences, on the smudge in the center of her handkerchief, and to the conversation with Piotr about the Namsat. When she looked up, he was gone.

"Jon! Where are you?" The gloom of the forest smothered her words, pushing them to the ground.

Why hadn't she paid attention? She must've slackened her pace when she was lost in her thoughts and fallen behind, and Jon, concentrating on the Path, had not thought to check that she was right behind him—as she should've been. What if she'd strayed from the Path?

If she had, then she was as lost as her thoughts.

Susan screamed herself hoarse calling for Jon, but it was no good. She was lost in the gloom. She sat down in a dejected heap, hunched her back and wept. At the touch of her tears dropping onto her hands, she stiffened. "No! I won't cry. Not these tears." She wiped her hands and face with her cape and sat in lotus. "I'll stay right here, and Jon will find me." She pulled the hood over her head and waited.

A tingling on her scalp suddenly made her alert. Out of the gloom, a dazzling white owl flew towards her on silent wings. Despite its large eyes and hooked beak, she felt no fear. It hovered in front of her face, sharp black talons extended from feet on the end of feathered legs, then alighted on her left shoulder.

The owl pulled her hood back and touched its beak to her ear. Susan's eyes widened as she heard its soft voice speak to her. She rose from her lotus and began walking with the white owl on her shoulder. When she emerged from the forest, she spotted Jon before he saw her.

"Your Souci! Thank the Giver you're safe. I

searched everywhere for you. I ran all the way back to the burnt field and couldn't find you anywhere. Where did you go? How did you find your way to the Path? I'm so happy to see you!"

She strode up to him.

"What's this?" He plucked a white feather from her shoulder and held out the white bit of down between his finger and thumb.

She took the small feather, touching it to her cheek before putting it in her bag. "One of my treasures."

"Your Souci, your face. It's..."

She touched her cheeks. "The Grime?"

"After Gyldfen scared us, it came back. I don't understand."

Susan did, but she didn't want to talk about it. Not yet. So she shrugged her shoulders. "Let's find a Path marker and walk."

CHAPTER TWELVE

THE FIELD OF WONDER

Before them a field stretched to the horizon, rippling with daisies and buttercups.

"Which way?" As she spoke, Susan felt a tingling at her feet. She looked down and saw she stood on a Path marker. Namsat? She tried to shake the thought away and focused on the marker. "Does the star look different to you?"

"A little, Your Souci. It seems fatter—the lines, I mean. It looks more like the kind of star I'd draw if you asked me to make one. Is that what you mean?"

Susan nodded. Then she stared across the endless field. "How are we going to take a bearing in all that emptiness?"

Jon scratched his head, then shrugged his shoulders. "I was hoping you might have an idea after you looked at the marker, Your Souci, because you knew what the zigzags meant on the last one."

Susan considered the ocean of meadow grass and flowers. "Perhaps we could wait till it's dark, and you could navigate by the stars. You know which is the star over the Rugged Mountains, right?"

"The Star of Gilead?"

"Yes."

"Not exactly, Your Souci. I'm more of a land sort of fellow, if you get what I mean. I've never really scanned the stars in a navigator's way because the sea and I don't get along, and fiddling with ropes and sails makes me feel like I'm in a huge tangle and nothing ever seems to go straight, what with the wind blowing in directions I don't want to go and the waves knocking me about. Don't get me wrong, Your Souci, I love stars, but they're beautiful things to me, like jewels scattered on a velvet cloth by a giant hand, and though I know the names of some, the ones that folks told me stories about, that made them into friends, like Velops and Mazon and Tion and... Now Mazon, there's a fellow. He wasn't even a star in the beginning but because—"

"Jon..."

"What? Oh, sorry, Your Souci. Anyway, I've left

the stars pretty much to themselves and didn't get to know them in a useful sort of way, you see, like Piotr with the Histories. I mean, how can you treat friends and beauties like tools? But as to Gilead, I have to confess I've never seen it nor met anyone who has, except maybe Piotr, and I'm not even sure he has because he's never said. All I know about Gilead is the riddle and a beautiful, sad story. So here I am at a disadvantage again and not a proper guide or much help and, well, wishing I'd studied more instead of wandering around and talking to people."

"You *are* a good guide. And what you do know must be more important than what you don't about those silly Histories and your beautiful stars. Traveling at night is probably not a good idea for some reason."

"There you go. I didn't want to mention it right off, Your Souci, but if a dragon's hunting you, walking in the dark isn't the best thing to do because you're going to need a light at some point, you see, and dragons have sharp eyes and a light, no matter how small, would be a beacon to Gyldfen and before we knew it, he'd be on us."

"Okay, then. Since night travel is what we shouldn't do, there must be some way to follow the Path across that field in daylight. We just need to think. Let's have a honey cake and do so."

They realized how hungry they were as soon as Susan uttered the words, and they both dove into their bags for food. Jon pulled out a honey cake first. Susan's hand found the white owl feather, distracting her.

"Mmm." Jon bit into the cake, dripping honey onto his beard. Then he noticed Susan wasn't eating anything. "Oh, I beg your pardon, Your Souci. Here, take mine."

But Susan ignored the honey cake, contemplating the feather. Removing the gold hoop from her left ear, she tried to puncture the quill and thread the hoop through it.

"Here, Your Souci, let me. Hold this."

She took the honey cake and, when he pulled a needle set out of his bag, gave him the earring and feather. While he worked she munched on the cake. When he handed her the earring with the feather securely threaded on the hoop, she reinserted the earring.

"It looks good, Your Souci. I bet Piotr would say there's a feather earring in the Histories and make you angry. I almost wish he were here just so I could watch you two argue again." He laughed. "It was as delicious as honey cakes!"

Susan smiled at her friend, then closed her eyes, listening to something else. "Spin me around, Jon. I want to see if it works."

"What?"

"Just spin me." She kept her eyes closed.

Jon put his hands on her shoulders and turned her around a few times. "Is that enough?"

"Good. Now check the Path marker and face the way it's pointing."

"Why?"

"Just do it, okay?"

"Yes, Your Souci."

"Have you done it?"

"Yes, I'm facing the right way."

"Good." Taking a deep breath, she rotated herself and then stood still. She turned her head a little and adjusted her body so that all of her faced the same direction. "All right, am I pointing the same way as the Path marker?"

Jon looked. "How'd you do it?"

Susan opened her eyes and checked for herself. "Good. It works."

"What does?"

"The White Owl's feather."

"That was a feather from the White Owl? The White Owl guided you out of the forest?"

"It seems," she said, " that we've been provided with another compass."

"How?"

It seemed obvious to Susan. The Namsat sent the White Owl, who guided her out of the Gloomy Wood she'd been lost in. The White Owl gave her one of its feathers to listen to in the same way she'd listened to the owl. All she had to do was hold the feather to her ear and pay attention. But because the feather was tiny and she might lose it, the best way to make sure she always had it was to attach it to herself. Thus the earring. Really, why was Jon being obtuse?

"Trust me, it just does," she said.

"Oh."

At first they stopped often to let Susan check their bearing with her earring. As she gained confidence, though, they stopped less frequently and walked further. By sunset they still couldn't see anything on the horizon. Nor could they see the gloomy forest. Infinite waves of grass and flowers flowed around them.

"Well, Jon, do we stop for the night or keep on?"

"My feeling is to stop, Your Souci, because we don't know how far we have to go before we're across. If we could see something that told us there's an end in sight, then of course we'd just keep going till we got there, but we don't and rest is important if we have to walk as far again tomorrow. I'm glad we're not lost because I could certainly feel lost in this forever field."

"So we stop. Do you have a tent in your bag of treasures?"

"Not that I know of, but I could check."

"I've got one."

"You do?"

Susan nodded. She'd been waiting for this moment since the Bumbles had shown her the wonder of her cape. She reached inside the cape and removed two little bundles of poles from the pockets on each side. "They're shock-corded. See?"

"Shock-what?"

"This." She showed him the little elastic cords inside the ends of the poles that held each set together. Most of the poles came in pairs and, when joined, formed longer poles. There was only one set of three.

"That's the ridge pole."

"Why are there extra holes in it?"

"The short ones go in them. Like this."

She stuck four of the two-pole lengths into the long pole to produce an A-frame skeleton.

"But where's the tent?"

"Here." She removed her cape. First she pulled out the shorter poles and threaded the long one through small loops in her cape. Then she threaded the shorter ones through other loops in the cape and re-attached them to the long pole. When she'd finished, a two-man tent stood before them.

"A cape-tent! What a perfect thing for rambling, Your Souci."

"The Bumbles showed me when I was changing back at Piotr's. The only problem is that there's no floor."

"That doesn't matter. I wonder if they'd make me one when we get back?"

"Of course they would. They're sweet dears. And now we can sleep in comfort and not worry about rain or dew. And I bet we can use our walking sticks to hold up the entrance flap if we want to look out at the stars."

Susan took their walking sticks and propped up the flap. Then she clambered into the tent. As Jon bent to follow her in, he was hit by a rock she tossed out. Then another.

"Wait, Your Souci. I'll help you."

"Where did all these rocks come from? I don't re-member stepping on any when we were walking."

Together they cleared the ground, ate another honey cake and drank from their water flasks. Then they settled down. Watching the Ebal sky sparkle with ever more stars as the night deepened, they speculated on which might be the Star of Gilead. They fell asleep be-fore they could agree on one.

When Susan woke the next morning, Jon was up

already, examining one of the rocks they'd thrown out of their tent. She hitched herself to the front of the tent and sat for a moment.

"Did you sleep well?" she asked.

"Like a badger in its burrow, Your Souci. I hope Sharon and Misha can make me a tent from my jacket— a cape isn't the thing for me. You don't mind a breakfast of honey cakes and water, do you?"

She shook her head. "Let me fold the tent first."

With the unhurried grace of an expert, Susan soon had the tent apart and was wearing her red cape again.

"I was thinking about these curious stones, Your Souci. They're heavier than most and see how smooth they are. But it's what they do when you hold them near your mouth and talk that's got me wondering."

Susan picked up a stone and held it in front of her mouth. She spoke a few words. "They vibrate!"

"There's something in the back of my mind about them that I just can't get to the front, something some-body told me long ago or I heard somebody talking about or something I read, though the Giver knows I haven't read much. But there's something, so I think I'm just

160

going to put this little fellow in my bag till I can remember."

Susan put one of the rocks in her bag too. Then she took their bearing with her feather earring. As they walked, they found themselves stepping on more and more of the curious rocks, tripping over the bigger ones. Not long after their lunch break Jon tripped for the third time. As he regained his balance and was about to go on, he stopped in mid-step.

"Your Souci! We're in the Field of Wonder! I never thought it was true, though I always hoped it was, and here we are right in the middle of it! To think I should live to find it and on the Narrow Path! This is just too glorious and I owe it all to you because if you'd never come and I hadn't opened the Gate, I'm sure I'd never have come this way or if I did I wouldn't have come so far, would I, because the field is just too wide and I couldn't cross it with no bearing to follow and I'd turn back, you see, when the gloomy forest was still in sight which would mean I wouldn't come to where all the rocks are, right here where we are now."

"Jon, please. Just tell me what the Field of Wonder is. Never mind the rest."

"I can't, it's too…" He produced a harmonica from his coat pocket and had it at his lips playing a song before Susan could say another word.

Within seconds she heard another instrument take up the melody, then another and another till the simple tune had become a symphony played by a ghostly orchestra hidden among the waving grass. Her eyes closed as she listened, entranced.

"Your Souci." Jon's voice seemed to come from a distant place.

When Susan opened her eyes, she looked into his tear-wet face. She heard only silence now and felt the coolness of a soft wind drying her cheeks.

"Oh, Jon! What was it? Where did that beautiful music come from?"

He held one of the stones. "In the beginning, the Giver made the Star of Gilead and the Star of Tessa. Together they sang stars into the sky and the sun and the moon. Then Ebal and the seas and trees. And mountains and fields and lakes and streams. Then all of the creatures and all of us. So everyone and everything is part of the great song. One day long, long ago, the Star of Tessa broke into pieces—no one knows why—and fell flaming to the ground, to here, Your Souci, and she lies scattered in the Field of Wonder. At the end of time, the Giver will sing Tessa together again and re-unite her with Gilead to sing forever. I can't keep a piece of Tessa in my bag of treasures, Your Souci, I can't break the hope of her rising."

Jon set the small rock he held on the grassy ground. Susan felt torn between wanting to keep hers as a memento of the story and leaving it in the field—what if the story were true?

"But why'd they sing when you played the harmonica?"

"Because a song, any song—even my poor playing of one—touches the memory of their wholeness and unites them again. That's what I was told. So perfect is their singing that my playing sounded like scratching to my ears and I had to stop to listen but, when I did, the song that re-connected them was over and they were broken again. It was so sad to hear the music die stone by little stone all over the field. I felt so alone when they stopped. And when I called you and you didn't open your eyes, I felt even lonelier. I'm so glad you're here, Your Souci." Then his eyes widened. "Your face—the grime's gone again! But why are your hands and hair still dirty?"

Before she could reply, the sky seemed to roar. "Gyldfen!" Susan tore across the field, feet flying over flowers and stones, Jon keeping frantic pace with her. A glance over their shoulders showed a dot of gold in the distance. But he had wings and they only legs to flee on.

"How…?" she panted.

"The song. He must've heard the song…"

On they ran, but closer came Gyldfen. Scanning the sea of grass for shelter, Susan spotted two little men running towards her and Jon, carrying what looked like a log.

"Hooray!" Jon shouted.

As the distance between them closed, Susan saw that what the beardless fellows carried now looked like a rolled-up carpet.

"Down!" Jon grabbed her and they fell to the ground. Moments later the little men reached them. They flung up the carpet and daylight vanished into darkness. Susan had time to hear the heavy breathing of four winded runners and Jon sigh, "Safe," before the first of Gyldfen's fire blasts burst on them—but harmlessly.

"Jon," she finally asked, "what is it and who are our rescuers?"

He found her hand and touched it to the wall of a dome enclosing them. "The Dragon Shield." He knocked on it with his fist. It rang like metal. "These are James and Zebedee, Carriers of the Shield."

A match flared in the dark and a candle lantern spread its light.

"James," said one.

Susan thought his boyish face looked Bumblish. He had their long, sad eyes that drooped at the corners. No orange fur, though.

"Zebedee," said the other, who looked identical to the first.

"Thank you, kind sirs," said Susan, "for coming to our rescue."

"All in the line," replied Zebedee.

"of duty," concluded James. "Glad to be,"

"of service," said Zebedee.

"They look like Sharon and Misha," whispered Susan to Jon.

"Cousins," he whispered back.

"What's a dragon shield? And where's the carpet they were carrying?"

Jon gestured to the dome covering them. "The carpet *is* the Shield, Your Souci. It's soft, you see, so it can be rolled up and carried, but when it's spread out in the presence of a dragon it hardens into this dome. No dragon fire nor dragon-tail blows can break the Shield. We're perfectly safe."

"Where'd they get it?"

"Legend says Camellia the Weaver, the first Queen of Ebal, made it when Gyldfen appeared for the first time. Ebal had gone wrong somehow, as Piotr explained—you know, it's funny how all the queens have to deal with Gyldfen—I never thought of that before—and…"

"What if Gyldfen just waits for us to come out?"

"Dragons aren't patient, at least that's what the stories tell, and when they're thwarted they go away to burn up other things. Like Gyldfen did to the meadow."

"Won't he come back?"

"We'll be gone by then and he'll have to find us again."

"How did the Carriers know we were here?"

"The Fairy Queen heard the singing," James answered.

"and sent us to find the new queen," Zebedee added, "because only she,"

"she said, would know the way across the Field of Wonder," said James.

"The Fairy Forest is nearby?" Jon asked.

"Only half," Zebedee began.

"a day's walk," finished James.

Jon's prediction about Gyldfen's impatience proved accurate. The blasting against the Shield soon ceased. Not long afterward Susan noticed the dome was beginning to sag. Then it collapsed and draped heavily on their heads. James snuffed out the candle and Zebedee lifted one side for Susan and Jon to wriggle out, followed by the Carriers, who began rolling up the Shield. When Susan turned her attention from searching the sky for Gyldfen, only a third of the carpet remained unrolled.

She was surprised to see the familiar design of circles disappearing in the rolls.

"Is this what's on the Shield?" She held her Bumble handkerchief open to the Carriers.

James and Zebedee glanced at it, nodded, and hoisted the Shield to their shoulders.

"Which," James asked, beginning the question.

"way?" said Zebedee, completing it.

"What's in the center of the design?" Susan asked.

"Same as," Zebedee started.

"the handkerchief," finished James.

The Carriers repeated their question.

"We must be going, Your Souci," Jon insisted.

"But...I need to understand. Don't you see it's part of the Path?"

So James and Zebedee told her.

"What!" Even Jon was surprised.

Susan pondered the knowledge in her heart.

"The bearing," James implored.

"Your Majesty," Zebedee concluded.

Susan closed her eyes and, shaking her head to feel the touch of the White Owl feather, pointed the way.

Staggering into the Fairy Forest a few hours after sunset, they fell asleep under the shelter of silver-grey trees.

CHAPTER THIRTEEN

THE FAIRY QUEEN

Susan woke in the milky light of pre-dawn, restlessness urging her to her feet. Jon, James and Zebedee slept without stirring. She was about to rouse them when a breath of wind brushed the White Owl earring against her skin. What now? Reluctant to leave her friends, she hesitated a moment, then set off into the forest of silver-barked beech trees, wondering what her destination was.

In a clearing, surrounded by a ring of fairies, stood the Fairy Queen wearing a crystal crown. Susan strained to keep the shimmering figure in focus, blinking quickly, then stretching her eyes wide. Nothing worked. Finally, she saw what caused the shimmering—the queen was facing all directions at the same time. "Nice trick." Susan watched from the edge of the clearing, ready to retreat behind a tree but not to go away; she felt something important was either happening or about to.

An exquisite voice began to sing. At first she

thought it was the Fairy Queen's, but when the crystal crown glowed like a miniature sun, followed by the first light of dawn piercing the forest, she was not all sure the crown itself wasn't singing. Though she saw the sun's light, the shadows from the trees faced away from the fairies. She realized the shimmering Fairy Queen was singing the dawn into being *through* her crown. The song lighted her crystal crown, which lighted the sun itself. Susan quivered to the Song of Dawn as though she were a piece of broken Tessa in the Field of Wonder.

Bubbling laughter burst from the fairies as they dispersed into the forest. The Fairy Queen alone remained and her shimmering slowed until she rested in perfect focus. She was silver-green, like the underside of a leaf. She looked at Susan.

"Now, my dear, what is this deception you've practiced on your friends?"

"I…I don't know what you mean."

"Come now, I'm not a Piotr full of stony words and hard demands. You're in Ebal because of your name, the name given to you because you are that name."

"But my name is Susan, not Camellia."

"And might your name be more than Susan?"

As she opened her mouth to deny it, Susan saw Jon watching her nearby—when had he appeared? She found herself unwilling to lie anymore.

"Yes, my name is Camellia too."

"Do you understand that even if you had owned your name at the start of your journey, you would still be on the Path?"

Susan nodded.

"Why do you think so?"

"Because…" Susan looked at Jon, his shapeless hat doffed in the queen's presence, "…I have to reach the Place of Choosing that the Gold Hall was only the entrance to."

"Very good. Now come here. I have a gift for you." In her hand lay a miniature of her crown.

"It's so beautiful!" Unlike the queen's crown, the miniature sparkled with a hint of gold. Susan hesitated to take it, fearful of breaking the delicate points.

"Don't be deceived, Susan Camellia. It's harder than a dragon scale."

When she had the little crown in her hand, Susan

noticed a tiny stopper in its center. "It's a little bottle."

"One day you may find a use for what it holds."

"Thank you, Your Majesty." Susan placed it safely in her bag. When she looked up, she saw only the forest clearing and Jon o'Gates. The Fairy Queen had vanished.

Jon broke the awkward silence. "What shall I call you now, Your Souci?"

Susan smiled at the little man who was becoming ever more dear to her. "What you've called me since we were in the mountain."

He considered a moment, then nodded his head, a sign that the matter was settled. "Right." He crushed his hat back on his head. "Let's find a Path marker, Your Souci, and get on our way."

"I think the Fairy Queen was standing on it."

"So she was. Well, here's our direction."

When they emerged from the Fairy Forest, the sun was low in the sky. Susan squinted at the distant horizon of a rolling, treeless expanse. "Is that…?"

"The Rugged Mountains!" Jon confirmed. "And this," he added, sweeping his arm over the miles of coarse grass, bracken and rocky outcroppings, "is the Zossen Moor. When I was a boy I wandered through it with my father—such a ramble that was!—the things he showed me, Your Souci—nothing to block our view of sky and mountains—little streams everywhere to fill our water bottles and catch fish in—berries galore—it's the perfectest place! And now I'm going with you!"

Susan smiled at her friend's enthusiasm. Casting a look into the Fairy Forest, she touched the silver bark of the tree beside her. "I'll miss their shelter, Jon."

"What's that?" He wrenched his gaze from Zossen and looked at Susan, her hand on the tree. He looked again at the moor. "Oh, I see. Good point, Your Souci—we'll be in the open all the way to the Rugged Mountains, and the only time Gyldfen's found us has been in the open."

"Perhaps one day there'll be time to return, and you can ramble it once more."

"Of course there will be. And won't we have a time!"

Susan felt a tug at her heart. What if she chose not to stay? "But right now we need a Path marker to take a bearing."

"Right as usual. The journey first. Let me just have a look around for the marker. It can't be far."

Susan stared into the distance, seeking an answer the rugged horizon didn't give her.

They hiked past sunset into darkness with no sign of Gyldfen. Susan pitched her cape-tent and their weary eyes dropped shut. They willed themselves awake before dawn so the dragon wouldn't catch them asleep in daylight. Day melted into day as the Rugged Mountains loomed ever larger, blocking more and more of the sky. Gyldfen didn't appear. Susan grew taciturn, feeling an invisible burden pressing her to slow down, whispering for her to stop. But she kept on, never slacking her speed, refusing to let Jon moderate his. At last they reached the mountains.

Susan had never seen anything like them. They sprang from the ground like trees. They were castle walls that shut out the sky, running in an unbroken line to the horizon on each side of her. "How do we get in?"

"Well, Your Souci, if the Narrow Path to the Star Flower leads to the Old One in the Rugged Mountains, then there must be a way. Piotr said he took his queen here, so the Path has to go in. Just because we can't see it right now doesn't mean it isn't here. I took our bearing on that overhang above us, and if you can't trust a Saluki compass, well, I ask you, what can you trust? There's a marker here all right and we'll find it, don't you worry. I'll keep a goose eye open for a bit of water as well—my flask's nearly dry and the mountains may not have the supply the moor does."

Susan was too tired to think about being thirsty.

Jon soon trotted back. "There's a stream a few paces away. C'mon, Your Souci, you'll feel as perky as a Bremen otter when you've had a good drink and splashed your face in cold water."

She kept her hot face in the stream as long as she could hold her breath. "Mmm. That feels good."

"Didn't I tell you?"

She plunged her whole head in, then shook like a dog when she raised it, her hair spraying water everywhere. "I think there's magic in the stream, Jon—I feel full of energy."

"Just what you need for the mountains, Your Souci.

177

Now, for that marker."

"Look in the stream for it," she suggested. When her head was underwater, she'd felt the Namsat tingling.

"The stream?" He pushed his face so close that his nose touched the surface. "You're right. How clever of you!" He turned his head to Susan, getting his ear wet. "The needle looks like a wavy line. What do you think?"

"Could the stream be the Path?"

They looked to where it issued from a crevice in the wall of rock.

"That crack isn't very high, Your Souci, and as much as I don't fancy wet boots, I believe if we were in the stream—wading, I mean—we just might be able to stoop low enough to get through. What am I saying? Of course we can fit—it's the Path. Ready when you are."

"What if the bottom drops away when we're inside the mountain?"

Jon shrugged. "Then we swim. In for a lantic, in for a tor, as my dad used to say. Hold the end of my stick so we won't be separated, Your Souci. No more gloomy woods and one of us getting lost."

Susan felt a tingle from her walking stick. "Could

we use mine, Jon?"

"The true stick. I should've thought of that. Sorry, Your Souci."

"It's like the mailbox tunnel," Susan muttered at the dark inside the crevice.

"You said something, Your Souci?"

"Just talking to myself." She was glad she could feel Jon at the end of her stick. "I hope Gyldfen isn't at the end of this."

"Me too." Jon had heard clearly this time.

When they waded into daylight again and straightened up, all thoughts of Gyldfen flew from their minds. They stood on the edge of a small lake at the bottom of a crater, whose walls towered thousands of feet above them. The waterfall that plummeted from the top of the crater became a plume of mist by the time it reached the lake. As they stared in awe, Susan felt the Namsat tingling. "It looks like a giant white feather," she said.

Her words triggered a line from Piotr's riddle: "...*the plume of white feather hair*," Jon recited. "We're here, Your Souci! We're here!"

She recalled the riddle Piotr had posed at the first

Path marker. "Where's the 'thirteenth flight of stairs'?"

"There!" Jon shouted.

A staircase rose from the lake, hewn out of the cliff face, weaving its way back and forth behind the falls. Susan peered up at it, counting the flights. "Eleven. There are only eleven! Five on that side and six on the other."

Jon counted and got eleven too. "Maybe we can't see the others from here. There's only one way to find out, Your Souci—climb. I'm game."

"Up we go, then."

They splashed across the shallow lake to the bottom of the stairs. The marker was on the first step and the vertical part of the second one. There was no doubting the direction of the Path—up. Their thighs burned by the sixth flight. At the start of the ninth, they were leaning heavily on their walking sticks.

"Rest, Your Souci?"

"We daren't. My legs are jelly. If we stop, we'll never start again. And I have to know about the thirteenth flight."

"Up we go, then. Thank the Giver for good sticks."

At the end of the eleventh flight, the twelfth angled

into the cliff itself. "You were right about us not seeing all the stairs," Susan said. "I bet the thirteenth set is at the end of the Path and leads to the Old One." Susan hurled herself into his arms, hugging him. "What would I have done without you? Piotr was right—there's no guide better than you."

"Your Souci!" Jon cried, collapsing under her sudden weight. They fell into a heap, laughing.

Then Susan became serious. "Forgive me, Jon, for being such an ungrateful companion. I've been a misery to you, my dear, kind, sweet Jon o'Gates." She held him by the sleeve of his baggy green coat as he began to squirm, trying to escape. "No, don't run away—you must listen." She shifted her hands to his shaggy head to stop him from shaking it in denial. "You're kind and gentle. Everybody loves you, even gruff old Piotr—and so do I—and not just because you love everybody. I won't let anyone call me Souci but you."

When Susan gave him the gift of her name, Jon stopped squirming.

"You'd do that for me?"

"Only you."

At that moment, Gyldfen's roar reverberated down the passageway. Squeaking in fright, Susan clutched Jon, just as she had on a different mountain in what seemed a lifetime ago.

"There, there, Your Souci." He stroked her grimy hair. "Gyldfen's too fat to fit into that passage. We're safe here." All the same, he kept a wary eye on the entrance for Gyldfen's shadow. If he saw it, he'd hustle Susan behind the damp protection of the waterfall.

No shadow came. Nor did Gyldfen repeat his roar. As Susan's shivering abated, Jon pondered that single roar. "I know this is hard to believe, Your Souci, but I think that was Gyldfen's death cry."

Still holding on to his coatsleeves, Susan pushed herself back from Jon and looked into his face. "He's dead?"

"I'm pretty sure. I'll just creep up the passageway and have a look-see."

"No!" Susan pulled herself back into his arms, tucking her head under his bearded chin and holding him tightly. "Don't leave me!"

"Of course not. There, there."

But once she'd heard the impossible, hoped-for death voiced, Susan couldn't banish the idea from her mind. What if it were true? She was supposed to slay Gyldfen herself, but if Jon said he was dead, maybe...

She summoned her courage. "Let's both go."

"What if I'm wrong?"

"Then you're wrong. I won't be left alone, Jon, so we either stay here forever, or I go with you."

"I guess we go."

When they reached the end of the passageway, they poked their timid heads out. Nothing. Cautiously, they walked into the open, then stared open-mouthed.

In the middle of the river, just before it hurled itself over the crater lip into the waterfall, the great golden dragon lay impaled on a solitary, needle-like spire of rock.

"He looks dead," Jon ventured.

Gyldfen's head faced them, dangling limply a few feet above a tumble of rocks that marched up the river from where he hung. His huge wings crumpled impotently around the piercing spire, and his legs rested in the river, their raking claws hidden below the surface. His sprawling body hid the long coil of his tail from their sight.

Disbelief numbed Susan's elation. Even as her eyes took in Gyldfen's huge carcass, her mind could not credit what they saw. Something more was needed to convince her. She spotted a canoe overturned on the bank in front of her.

"I have to touch him."

She dashed to the canoe, expertly flipped it, pushed it into the river and, clutching her walking stick, jumped in.

"Your Souci! Come back!"

She dropped her stick in the boat and picked up the paddle, drove it into the river and held it there, leaning out over the river. Seconds passed as she drifted downriver, holding her position. At last the canoe swung around and swept downstream towards Gyldfen and the waterfall. She back-paddled furiously, slowing the canoe. As she approached the dragon, she plunged in the paddle again, leaning her body so far out of the tilted canoe that only her legs remained inside. She floated towards Gyldfen.

"You'll go over the falls," Jon whimpered.

But the canoe pivoted, coming to rest in the eddy created by the rock just upstream of Gyldfen's head. Bless Aunt Camellia and white water canoe training. Waving to Jon from her perch in the canoe, she tilted back her head and looked up. Her arm froze above her, pointing at Gyldfen's gaping mouth.

CHAPTER FOURTEEN

CAMELLIA THE BALD

She heard a gurgle echo inside the dragon. Screaming, "He's alive!" she scrambled out of the canoe and onto a rock. A belch of fire poured from Gyldfen's yawning jaws, his horrid tongue uncoiling in the midst of the flames. The canoe burned up in an instant. Fire enveloped Susan.

The hood of her cape, which had been pulled over her head, was incinerated. Her hair shriveled into ash and drifted away. Seeing her walking stick floating intact, she dashed her hand into the water and retrieved it. She noticed her hand was clean, looked at the other and found the fire had cleansed it of the Grime too. Feeling a sudden coldness on her head, she raised her hand inquiringly. Naked skin: she was bald.

Not a thread of the hair her mother had gloried over remained. "So much for a buzz cut," Susan laughed. Suddenly she realized she'd been cleansed of all the

Golden Grime. And Gyldfen was taken care of once and for all, just as Queen Beatrice had asked. Susan pirouetted on the rock. "I'm free and clean!"

Standing on tiptoe, she stretched her arm up to Gyldfen. Stone cold. She stepped back to examine what she could see of the carcass. His tongue looked like a charred piece of meat—streaks of red in the midst of black. Staring at the tongue in sudden recognition, she held her stick next to it. The same pattern. "Well, stick, your name's Dragon Tongue."

A red sparkle on the rock at her feet caught her eye. Picking up the large ruby, Susan felt the Namsat tingling. She looked at the dragon's head and saw the empty eye socket. Turning to the ruby, she peered into it. Like a flaw at the center of the jewel, a miniscule dragon lay in wait. "And that's where you'll stay, my friend." She pulled the Bumble handkerchief out of her bag and compared the dragon in the ruby to the smudged image at the center of the labyrinth design. "So James and Zebedee were right. Gyldfen." She wrapped the ruby in the handkerchief and put it in her singed bag.

The outer layer of her cape had burned away, but

the inner one with its tent loops remained intact. The pockets and poles had survived too.

"All in all, I'd say I'm in pretty good shape for a dragon survivor."

Susan looked across the river at Jon and shouted that she'd been cleansed of the Grime, but the noise of the waterfall drowned her words. Jon yelled himself voiceless telling her he'd seen what had happened and to look for a Path marker. She shook her head to let him know she didn't understand. "Well," she said to herself, "now what?" She didn't like being separated from Jon. "How am I going to get back without a canoe?"

Jon waved and gestured upstream, taking a few steps that way, urging Susan to go up there to find a marker. He'd seen one where the canoe had been, pointing across the river. Maybe the noise of the waterfall would be lessened there and they could hear one another. She turned her back on Gyldfen and walked to the end of the spine of rocks but still couldn't hear Jon. The White Owl earring brushed against her skin. "Right, the marker. How stupid of me. Bless you, Jon, for remembering the journey." She blew him a kiss. Jon waved his hat in acknowledgement.

On the rock nearest the opposite shore she found the Path marker, its needle pointing across the river. She noticed six faint circles on the needle. "What does that mean?" She looked back at Jon and signaled her find. Then she focused on the task at hand: getting across to find the Old One.

Susan squinted at the river, straining to see through it until her eyes watered and she had to look away. The walking stick sent a tingle through her hand. "Okay, Namsat, how does Dragon Tongue help me across?" Stepping to the edge of the rock, water lapping at her boots, she thrust the stick into the river. The current nearly swept it out of her hand. She gauged the length of her stride and thrust the stick into the water that distance away. Her stick hit a rock no more than an inch below the surface. The rapid flow of the river had prevented her from seeing it. But even though she knew the rock was there, Susan was not comfortable trusting something she couldn't see, especially when it was in the middle of a rushing river.

"Before I take that step, I think I need to feel calmer

than I do now." She closed her eyes, placed her right foot on her left thigh and put her hands in prayer pose. Then she stretched her arms above her head, fingers pointing to the sky. She began ujjay breathing, concentrating until all she heard was the sound of her breath rasping over her palate. Tree pose. A minute later she lowered her arms, dropped her leg, and opened her eyes. She stepped into the river.

Her foot came down on an unmoving rock. She thrust her stick and found the next stone on her first jab. Susan walked across the river on six stepping stones. "Six circles," she said when she stood on the shore.

From his place on the other side of the river, Jon had seen something he could hardly believe. "Her Souci walked on water!"

Susan spotted the marker immediately, its needle pointing downstream to a path that angled away from the river and into a wood. Daylight was fading. Would there be time to find the Old One? According to Jon, this was the thirteenth day of their journey and, though no one had said how much time she'd been given to complete it, Susan sensed she only had thirteen days. She turned and waved once more to Jon o'Gates. Was this farewell?

Twilight made the wood gloomy. Recalling the time she'd got lost, Susan attended to the path and the path alone. She walked into a clearing and found the marker. But it had no direction needle and no mountain symbol, only the Star Flower—she'd reached the end of the Path. "So where's the thirteenth flight of stairs and the Old One?" she asked.

In the center stood a circular holly hedge, bright with red berries. The Namsat tingled when she walked up to it. She stared at the dense wall of prickly leaves. "Now what?" She began to circle the hedge. On the opposite side she found an entrance and stepped in. Her forward progress was instantly blocked by another wall of holly, forcing her to choose left or right. "Right, then." She slipped around the curve to find a dead end. She returned to the entrance, went left, and again found she had to make a choice between a right and left path. Realizing she was in a maze, she laughed. "Of course. Where else would the Old One be?" Twilight dropped into night. "And now it's dark as well."

Susan touched her White Owl earring. "It seems it's up to you now." Then she smiled to herself. "And me too, I guess." Despite listening as intently as she could, she frequently bumped into the maze's prickly walls. By the time she reached the center, her hands and bald head were bleeding from innumerable stinging scratches.

A gleaming crystal sphere as high as Susan sat in the middle of the maze. Touching its cool, smooth surface was a relief to her sore hands. She rested her cheek on it. As she did so, the crystal began to glow. Startled, Susan stepped back. She wasn't sure who she'd been expecting the Old One to be—an old man, perhaps, but not a crystal ball.

She saw a distorted image of herself reflected in the polished exterior, reminding her of the frightened, grimy one she'd seen in the glassy floor of the Gold Hall. She circled the sphere, her unreal reflection keeping pace. Thinking that the Old One might be inside, like Gyldfen in the ruby, she cupped her hands on the crystal and peered in. Her own eyes stared back. She blinked and focused behind those eyes, determined to see. And then she did.

She watched an old hag materialize and then change into an image of herself as she'd been in the Gold Hall, but now she wore a crown of black fire. She climbed onto Gyldfen's back and rode into the night until she transformed back into the hag. Then Susan saw the old woman shift into another image she recognized as herself, but clean and clear. Now she wore a golden crown exactly like the Fairy Queen's and sat on a red velvet throne, her walking stick in her hand. She waved her stick like a wand and vanished. The hag reappeared, looking steadily at Susan with Susan's own eyes until Susan pulled back from the crystal with a cry, dropping her walking stick. The crystal's glow faded.

Agitated, she began to pace around the sphere, trying to think but haunted by what she'd seen. In an effort to calm herself, she counted her steps, forcing her mind to attend to the mechanical exercise. When she reached her stick, she started again. By her twelfth circuit, she was calm, and at the end of her thirteenth, she stopped, knowing what she would do.

She took the Fairy Queen's gift from her bag and

removed the tiny stopper. Holding it directly over her head, she poured out the golden liquid, rubbing it all over her baldness. She rubbed the surprising amount of residue into her hands, and felt the stinging leave her scratches. "There," Susan said to the crystal ball. "I've chosen."

When a glow appeared above her reflection, she thought the Old One had something more to impart and bent towards the crystal. But then she noticed that the light didn't emanate from within the ball. It was her own head that glowed like a harvest moon. In the radiance of her golden head, Susan retraced her steps to the river and Gyldfen.

Jon o'Gates woke before dawn and paced the riverbank, searching the other side of the river for Susan. As he approached the lip of the falls, light shone from the crater, brightening quickly. He covered his eyes to protect them from the growing intensity, but the brilliance soon forced him to face upstream. When the momentary effulgence had dimmed, replaced by the soft pre-dawn light, he looked up at the brightest star he'd ever seen. "The Star of Gilead!"

Thoughts of the star's glory were pushed aside by the words of the ancient riddle. "It's risen!" Looking at the Gyldfen-killing spire, he noticed a golden glow radiating from the base of it. "And there's the 'golden needle'!" Within the nest created by the crumpled dragon wings Jon noticed what appeared to be a golden ball. As he strained to see it clearly, the sun crested the horizon. "Your Souci!" he cried.

Susan sat on Gyldfen's back, her bald head as golden as the dragon had been when he was alive. In her red cape, she rose from her lotus like a phoenix.

"Your Souci!" Jon called out again. She waved and blew him a kiss. "Hooray!" he shouted. "You're here, you didn't go!" Moments later a flock of Blue Ebal Geese surrounded him, full of cheerful honking.

Queen Beatrice landed beside Susan on Gyldfen. "We came as soon as we saw Gilead rise, Your Majesty. It's been a long time since I've laid eyes on that handsome fellow, yes it has. I see you've taken care of golden boy. A better job than Camellia the Green's too! I don't think he'll be sneaking off this rock the way he did from the Gold Hall."

Beatrice trained her bright eyes on Susan and arched her neck into a feathered hoop, running it over Susan's head.

"Just checking, Your Majesty. I didn't think you were hiding the grimy mess you had under a bald wig, but it's always best to be sure of the real thing, isn't it? That's certainly one way to fix bad hair or get rid of Golden Grime. Bit more radical than I had in mind, though. How'd you come by the golden glow?"

"The Fairy Queen."

"Traveling in high society now, are we? The Fairy Queen's a very nice girl, but she doesn't have a lot of focus. Good for sunrise, I'll admit."

Beatrice flicked Susan's earring with her beak. "This I like. Your own creation or a gift?"

"A bit of both. The White Owl gave me the feather, and Jon helped me put it together."

"First the Fairy Queen and then the White Owl herself! Honk my tail feathers, Your Majesty! But really, Jon can sew? A Keeper of many talents, he is. I always have the time of day for his sort, which is in far too short a supply, if the truth be known."

"The best in Ebal. I plan to keep him close by."

"Wise decision. You couldn't find better. The Bumbles gave you the key?"

"The dragon one?" Susan recalled the Namsat tingling she'd felt when she first handled it in her Bumble bag.

"That's it. You'll need it for the Return, but then I imagine you already know that."

Susan nodded.

"And the jewel? You've managed to pick one up, have you?"

"A ruby."

"First rate! I do like the way you're managing things right from the start. Saves a lot of time later."

"I hope so."

"Has the mark appeared?"

"You mean this?" Susan untucked her shirt and exposed her stomach. Decorating it was a tattoo of the labyrinth design she'd first seen on the Persian carpet her Aunt Camellia had sent her.

"That's the one." Beatrice raised a webbed foot and brought it down on Gyldfen. "The reason for ending up on golden boy?"

"The 'thirteenth flight'."

"Never cared for numbers myself. But then the patterns show up better from the air, so their numbers don't seem quite as important. Well, I think that should do it. Always like to catch up on the gossip. Pleasure before duty. Are you ready for the flight, Your Majesty?"

"I thought I'd fly on my own, if you don't mind."

"What! With one little ear feather?"

"No. On something the Bumbles created. I figured it out after Gyldfen delivered his final burn."

"Those Bumbles! I thought they couldn't do anything to surprise me anymore, but now they're building wings! Orange fur balls of mystery, they are. Full of astonishments. Probably comes from not talking much, that's my view. Always keep things close to the flight feathers. I'll fly a close escort, if you don't mind, Your Majesty. Experts are good to have nearby in case of trouble."

"That's kind of you, Beatrice. I'd be honored to have you near."

"Of course, of course. Time to stretch the wings, eh?"

"Do you suppose you might carry Jon yourself? It would mean a great deal to me to know he's in the best of wings."

"Had the same thought myself, Your Majesty. Don't you worry, I'll give him a good flight."

"Thank you. I'll need a few minutes to put my wings together."

"It'll probably take that long to clean the muck off Jon's boots. If one doesn't look after one's own feathers, who will? Just you go ahead when you're ready–I won't be far behind. Oh, one last thing. What made you choose to stay?"

Susan smiled. "I learned to be who I am."

"Couldn't have put it better myself." The royal goose spread her blue wings and glided down to Jon.

At the base of Gyldfen's tail, Susan stared into the depths of the crater, feeling the earthward tug great heights always created in her. Then she walked down the dragon tail, accordioned into steps from his death throes—the thirteenth flight of stairs she'd ascended when she reached the river after leaving the Old One. As quickly as she'd made a tent out of her cape, she now snapped the poles together to fashion a hang glider, missing only a cross-brace at the bottom to keep her legs up. Her stick, Dragon Tongue, provided that. Standing on the diamond tip of Gyldfen's tail, she leaned forward and dropped over the cataract.

Moments later Susan swooped out of the crater, spiraled heavenward on red wings, her bald head flashing gold as she contemplated Gyldfen impaled on the spire. "He looks like the star on the Narrow Path markers and the flower of the Saluki compass," she thought.

As the Namsat directed her towards Ingersoll, the geese joined her, carrying Jon the same way they had when they'd fled Mt. Gylla. "Your Souci!" he called. "Queen Beatrice says you did slay Gyldfen. But how?"

Beatrice honked the answer for Susan, paying Jon her highest compliment. "With love, you dear goose, with love. All the rest is Golden Grime."

Thus began the glorious reign of Camellia the Bald,

fondly remembered, even in the Histories, for her zig-zagging rambles with Jon o' Gates across the Queendom of Ebal.

The Old Made New

Susan stepped out of her aunt's fireplace and into a life she wasn't sure she wanted to take up again. She saw she was wearing her T-shirt, jeans and tennis shoes. The Bumble bag hung from her shoulder. Shaking her head, she felt the White Owl earring still in place—and something else too. She touched the short curly hair on her head, not displeased with the discovery.

"Darling!"

She stared at her aunt. "Why aren't you old or dead?"

"How could I be, darling?" Aunt Camellia laughed. "You've only been gone for two hours."

Susan's eyes met her aunt's.

"Two hours," she repeated. "But…" She'd been in Ebal for decades! When she'd received the Dream of Return and journeyed with Jon to Mt. Gylla, she'd been an old woman. Back in the Golden Hall, she'd inserted the dragon key into the Gate of Going and walked down the long tunnel to the fireplace. How could only two hours have passed?

"Many treasures can be found on a beach walk," her aunt prodded.

Susan sensed the test. It was almost as if she were back in Piotr's house. She held out her hand, fingers down, and noticed she wasn't wearing her ring. Hoping it was in her bag, she rummaged through her treasures. Aunt Camellia edged forward as Susan pulled out her hand, closed in a fist. When she opened it, her coronation ring sparked its fire from the ruby that had once been Gyldfen's eye and now was his prison.

Aunt Camellia threw open her arms. "Welcome home, darling." Susan hesitated a second, then ran into them.

"Oh, Aunt C., I don't know if I'm glad to be back."

"Of course not, Sue C. How could you?"

They pushed back from their embrace, looking at one another.

"Sue C.?"

"Aunt C.?"

"Did Papa tell you that?"

"No, it sprang to my lips just now. Why did you call me Aunt C.?"

Susan shrugged. "It seemed right."

"Given that we've spontaneously assigned each other special names, one might assume a special relationship exists between us."

"Besides Ebal and the Namsat?"

"At the very least, I dare say. Now, you must let me sketch you—my fingers simply won't wait. Scruggs'll make us mint tea and you can tell me everything while I work."

"You'll talk too, won't you, Aunt C.? There's so much I want to know."

"Naturally, which is why I need something for my hands to do—to help my mouth from overflowing. Just let me attend to the tea. You wait right here."

Susan looked around the hall that seemed a distant memory. The figures on the gold shield no longer had the power to mesmerize her. How could they? She'd been queen of them all. She slipped the ruby ring onto the finger where it had sat since her reign in Ebal had begun.

207

"There, that's taken care of," Aunt Camellia said upon her return. "Now to the studio and business, shall we?" She slipped her arm around Susan's waist and Susan did the same to her aunt. "I take it from your ruby ring that your title was Camellia the Red."

"To match yours as the Green? I tried, Aunt C., but…well, once I arrived at Ingersoll there didn't seem to be any doubt I would be the Bald."

"The Bald!" She ruffled Susan's crop of curls. "I can scarcely imagine—you must explain. I can hardly wait to see my sketch of you as you were. Half a moment, I've just had the most delicious idea! I'll sketch your entire adventure and work up the more compelling pieces into paintings. Yes, that's what we'll do. My fingers are itching to get started."

"May I have the sketches when you're done, Aunt C.?"

"Certainly, darling. It's your story after all. I do hope I have enough paper on hand. Yes, of course I do. How fortunate I bought that box before you arrived today. Now I know why. It's the most marvelous souvenir, you know, that the Namsat works here, although there's a different agenda."

"What do you mean?"

"We're ex-queens, aren't we, darling? And since we no longer reign, isn't it logical to assume our purpose within the Namsat is different too?"

"So what is our purpose?"

"Ah, there's the issue, isn't it? But more of that later. Right now, we have work to do and your story to hear."

All the studio walls except the one that joined it to the house were glass. Even the sloping roof was glass. Soft Carolina light washed through the room, muting the clutter of small tables haphazardly piled with paper, rolls of canvas, pots of brushes, boxes of pencils, tins and tubes of paint speckled with color, and unframed paintings leaning against table legs and one another.

"It's wonderful, Aunt C."

"It does the trick. Saw something quite similar when I was in Sicily. It didn't have the glass roof, though. Amazing how similar our quality of light is to the Mediterranean's."

"You must see all the stars in here."

"Not quite, as you'll discover tonight. And after Ebal, they're just not as good. To feel more at home, I painted the Ebal stars and constellations on the glass with iridescent paint. It's quite spectacular. And our stars shine through as well, which gives an added effect."

"You have Gilead?"

"Tessa too."

"You saw Tessa?"

"I can only wish. I painted what I imagined she'd look like beside Gilead."

"I held a piece of her when I crossed the Field of Wonder with Jon o' Gates."

"I envy you that. I'm afraid Piotr got us lost and we missed the Field of Wonder. Thank goodness the Namsat got us back on the Path. Did you get to Nine Beaches for the sunset?"

Susan raised her hand to her mouth in shock. "Oh, no!"

"What—something about Nine Beaches?"

"No, the Tessa stone—I never put it back. I brought it with me! What am I going to do, Aunt C.?"

"I'm afraid there's nothing you can do. Not at the

210

present, at least. Calm yourself, Sue C. We'll talk about it another day. Just find a stool—there must be one somewhere—and perch yourself on it. I'll fetch what I need to begin."

"But…"

"Trust me, darling, it'll all work out, I promise. Right now, I need you to pose."

Susan saw there was nothing to do but go along with her aunt. The stools all had paintings propped against them. She picked the one with the fewest, moved them against other paintings and climbed up. "Is this okay?"

"Perfect. First tell me how you came to be bald."

So Susan began her tale out of sequence. Aunt Camellia constantly interrupted her, forcing her to backtrack or jump to later events to satisfy her curiosity. When Scruggs announced dinner, Susan felt her memory was as jumbled as her aunt's studio.

"I'm not sure what I've told and what I haven't."

"No matter, Sue C. We have weeks to get it organized again. What you haven't said is how you got into Ebal."

"Through the mailbox at the end of the bridge."

"Mailbox? I don't suppose it matters—I'm quite sure it won't be there now. Still, going to check will give us an excuse to take an after-dinner walk."

"You promised me a swim too."

"Such a good memory you have for an old woman, Sue C."

They laughed.

"I still want to go swimming," Susan insisted.

"Did you bring a bikini?"

"I just bought it."

"Pity."

"Why, what's...?" Then Susan remembered. She pulled up her shirt. The tattoo was still on her stomach. "Doesn't it go away?"

"It fades and grows smaller, but it does remain. Look." She showed Susan hers. "Mind you, with the current rage for tattoos, we might find ourselves quite in fashion. I could add a sketch of it to the collection. And the mailbox. Such a droll idea, quite Ebalish, I'd say. As if you were a package being sent."

"I was in a way," Susan countered. "You and the

Namsat sent me. How did you go, Aunt C.?"

"Sailing in Sicily. A little squall blew up and when it was over, there I was, sailing into Port Saluki."

"Can anybody go to Ebal? I mean, do you have to be named Camellia just to go? Couldn't a man like Papa at least visit?"

"It's a gray area," Aunt Camellia hedged. "I'm sure we'll get into it before you leave."

"Well, when I get married and have a son, his middle name will be Camellia too so that he can go."

"But you won't, you see."

"I can name him whatever I want."

"Not that. Getting married, I mean, and having children. Queens of Ebal never marry or have children. We're always aunts. It's the price we pay, I'm afraid."

"That's hardly fair."

"But then, what is, Sue C.?"

Two weeks later, with her sketches done, Aunt Camellia ushered Susan into the only locked room Susan had come across in the mansion. Her aunt had always deflected her questions about it. In the small room, she found a compact library of ancient books. She instantly recognized the book on the solitary table.

"How did you get a copy of the Histories?"

"From the Camellia before me. It's the Queen's copy, which one day I'll pass on to you."

"Why?"

"Many reasons, darling. One of the most fascinating. Do you see how some of the pages are uncut, unable to be read? Well, in those pages you'll one day read who the next Camellia is and how you're to train her."

"You'll help me, won't you, Aunt C.?"

"I doubt whether an ex-Queen of Ebal needs help with anything the Histories have to say—think of dear old Piotr. Don't worry, my dear, when it's time, you'll be ready. If you like, you may spend the morning in here flipping through the book. There are some particularly fascinating passages about the Gates you asked about. And after today, you won't see the book again till your aunthood arrives."

"There are Gates, then! That's how I can return the Tessa stone. And Dinkins and Scruggs came through one, didn't they? I bet they're cousins to the Bumbles."

"No more questions, darling. Do you want to read

the book?"

"Yes, a thousand times yes! Lock me in here for the morning if that's all the time I have to learn about the Gates. Go, go, let me read."

A week later, when Susan heard her father's voice on the phone, she knew it was time to go home.

"Would you care to leave your treasures here with me, for safe-keeping?" Aunt Camellia asked.

"Thank you. I was hoping I could. But I want to take my Bumble bag."

"Of course. Since it could pass for a bag bought at a craft show, it'll raise the fewest suspicions."

"I'll miss you, Aunt C."

"I'm sure I can purloin you away during your holidays, not to mention special trips abroad we can arrange. You'll need a great deal of training to be a fit aunt, you know. It's not like being Queen of Ebal."

Thoughts of her irascible mother filled Susan's mind on the flight home. If that's what happened when you became a mother, she decided, maybe being an aunt wouldn't be so bad. Poor mother. If only she could change back to who she was before her head began to hurt. If Piotr had changed, couldn't she?

She was surprised when her father met her at the airport, alone. "Where's Mom?"

"At home, Sue C. She's been a little under the weather." In the car he mentioned his trip to France had been cut short.

"I'm sorry, Papa. How long have you been back?"

"Two weeks."

"Why didn't you call me? I would've come home."

"I know, Sue C., but Aunt Camellia and I felt it was probably better that you stay with her, given the circumstances."

"What circumstances?" She felt a sense of foreboding. "Why did you come back from France? It's Mommy, isn't it?"

"Yes, at least…it was, but everything's fine now. You'll see."

"What happened, Papa? Tell me! Did she have an accident? Is she in a coma? What?"

"Reste calme." Be calm. "Mommy's doing won-

derfully. You'll be so happy."

"Papa! Tell me what happened. You're as bad as Jon o'Gates."

"Who? Never mind. You remember I said she'd been getting confused and angry for a long while...?"

Susan nodded.

"And I'd wanted her to see the doctor, but she wouldn't?"

"Yes, yes."

"Well, she collapsed when I was in France. She had a seizure and they had to operate. That's why I rushed back."

"And you're sure she's all right?" Susan wanted her to be better, to be herself, a real mother.

"She's becoming more like her old self—the real old self—every day."

"I'm glad, Papa. Why did she have a seizure? What caused it?"

"Remember how I said she was worried about going insane because some of her relatives had died in asylums in the past? And that I wondered whether their insanity might've been misdiagnosed? Well, it turns out your mother had a brain tumor. As it grew over the years, it pressed on parts of her brain and caused her symptoms. It finally reached the point where it caused her seizure, which got her to the hospital and the doctors. And thanks to them, we have her back home and healing. When she asked me to call you, I did. She wants to see you, Sue C. She really loves you, you know. As much as I do."

The car hadn't come to a stop in the driveway before Susan dashed from it and raced into the house. Mrs. Cardiff was standing in the center of the Persian carpet. The coffee table and its ornaments had been banished. Her wispy hair had not grown back very far yet, but she wasn't wearing any of the bandages Susan had imagined. A beautiful smile played on her face.

"My darling Susan, you're home. Come here and let me hold you."

Susan melted into her mother's arms, crying. "I'm so sorry I was mean to you."

"There, there, Susie. I'm sorry too. I must've been horrible."

When she felt her mother kiss the top of her head, she wished she were bald again.

The End

Since he was a child, Tom Fleming has always known that he wanted to be an artist. He received his BFA from the School of Visual and Performing Arts at Syracuse University. In 1990, he became an artist/designer for the World Wrestling Federation. After three and a half years, he decided to return to freelancing. He began working with DC and Marvel Comics illustrating characters such as Superman, Spiderman, The Incredible Hulk, The X-men, and all his favorites. In 1995, Tom moved to Wilmington, NC, where he now resides and works out of his home studio. He has also started his own business creating and producing a line of figurines called "Tusslin' Bears."

E.W. Zrudlo lives in the historic district of downtown Wilmington, North Carolina, where he likes to wander around and talk to people. Writing keeps him from being too much of a pest. He is currently working on an account of his five-hundred mile walk through northern Spain along El Camino, the ancient pilgrimage route. Before settling in Wilmington—welcomed by a spate of hurricanes—he taught English and Classics at a private school in Canada. His three children are grown; his wife is deceased. He has published two ESL texts and a raft of poetry. *Camellia the Bald* is his first children's novel.

Saluki
Harbour

Camellia
the Green's
Castle

Mt. Gylla

The Gloomy
Forest

Goose
Bay

Ironwood

Field of Wonder

Piotr's House